• MAYURA AMARKANT
• JANELLE GIANNE
• KAINA LISIBACH • KEANU JOAQUIN DEL TORO •
• KALIVICTORIA WILSON • MONICA SINGH •
• KIM RASHIDI • TERRY LANDER •

STORIES FROM THE

Forest

10 STORIES OF NATURE, LOVE, LOSS AND LIFE

EDITED BY FLOR ANA
ILLUSTRATED BY KIM RASHIDI

Contents

Acknowledgments

This book was born from the idea of gathering authors and writers from all over the world to create a different kind of anthology. One filled with stories perfect for the spooky season, written with love. From gathering the stories and trying to figure out time zones to communicating through the internet and putting together this book, I'm grateful to have met all of these wonderful writers. It's been an amazing journey and I hope you love these stories as much as I do.

Thank you to Kim Rashidi for the wonderful and beautiful illustrations. Thank you to the amazing authors of this book for trusting me and for being the incredible, talented and kindhearted beings they are. Dalila, Janelle, Kaina, Kali, Keanu, Kimmy, Mayura, Monica, and Terry, you're all so wonderful and I look forward to an opportunity to work with you all again.

Thank you to my family, always, for the love and support with everything I do. And thank you to the readers, all across the world. May these stories carry on in your hearts.

— Flor Ana, editor

Viridian

By

Janelle Giannetta

As my right hand grazes the ground, I can feel the cool, soft grass between my fingers while they move. As my left hand reaches out to the side, it's automatically met with the sensation of an array of soft little petals surrounding a fuzzy center, something I imagine in my head to look like a sunflower.

Tapping into my other senses, my hearing quickly picks up the sound of a faint buzz. As it grows closer, it becomes a fast flapping of wings; the sound of summer: dragonflies. As they soon pass, my left ear heightens in on scattered, quiet chirping. Right away, I know this isn't any ordinary bird, but a hummingbird. In the distance, I can hear the high-pitched sounds of grasshoppers all around, which, in a way, soothes me. Somewhere close, I hear the sound of a branch breaking, most likely from a deer trotting in the woods. As I take a deep breath, the smell of the wilderness consumes me. The odor of pine from tall trees, clean air, and the fresh scent of bark all smell like home. Hidden behind the musky scent of the outdoors lies the strawberry scent of my long and luscious brown and wavy hair.

Finally, I decide it's time to open my eyes. The fluttering of eyelashes in front of my vision quickly turns into a bright, clear, turquoise sky, not one cloud in sight. In my peripheral vision, the color viridian engulfs me. From the numerous trees, bushes and plants, to the grass and the morning sky, my sight is clouded by various hues of greens and blues.

To my right, two bunnies frolic across the meadow. To my left, squirrels chase each other up a tree. While bees buzzing near me would normally frighten me, at this moment, I am completely unbothered. Much to my surprise, a ladybug, Miss Ladybug, decides to hang out on my pointer finger. She takes her time examining my skin as she crawls down my hand, twisting her way around to stop at my palm.

She waits a few seconds before lifting her wings and fluttering away. A sign of good luck, I suppose.

Just me, alone in nature, is exactly what I need. Time to appreciate all of the beauty that mother earth has so graciously bestowed upon us. Time to be alone with my thoughts and allow them to flow rather than consume me. Time to be present in the world as much as the moment will let me. Alone, but not lonely. Not here. How could I be? I have everything that I need in nature: the animals, the plants, the insects. I am simply soaking up all of the green surrounding me, and all of the light the sun allows me to. A quiet place. A safe place. That is what home is to me: nature. Not a care in the world, except making sure to notice all of the wonder around me. Surrounded by life and love.

Suddenly, something wet hits my cheek. A fragile wetness that makes one calm when outside instead of scurrying for cover. The type of wetness that makes you wonder where it could have come from. A soft drop, and a smooth wipe of the hand to make it go away.

I look up and see a few white clouds, the type that let you know they are not here to stay long, have decided to join me. The sky surrounding them is still a magical blue color. It is simply a rest stop for them to stay a few moments before passing by.

One drop, two drops, three. Nothing more than a gentle landing at most. A landing that started on my face, but is now trickling down to the rest of my body.

A feeling of joy rushes over me.

A sun shower! Oh, how I love them.

Sun showers are my favorite thing about the weather. It amazes me how it could be so charming out, sun shining down, yet rain could still peacefully fall from the sky, living together in harmony. Something I wish would happen more often on this earth. How could I be so lucky to experience such a powerful thing? Perhaps, it was that ladybug, or, perhaps, it was just nature thanking me for enjoying all that it has to offer. No matter what it is, a smile rises from my lips, beaming from one ear to the other.

As I lay here in this meadow, surrounded by sunflowers and creatures of all sorts, I think to myself how beautiful it is to be blessed with such natural art, how the world feels like it can just stop for a minute to let whomever enjoy such exquisiteness. Watching the rays of the sun and the rain from the clouds play together has to be the truest form of love there is, like how it feels to see day and night mix together when the sun is setting but the moon has already risen.

This world enchants me. I'll never understand how nature can be so alluring and fascinating at the same time. All thanks to our mother. She truly has done such a great job. I sit still, closing my eyes to enjoy the moment. Letting the rain absorb into my skin while the sun tries to melt it away.

I am joined by a friend. Miss Ladybug has come back to share this moment with me. Together, we patiently wait. We listen to the world around us. The sound of the rain landing on the leaves is something that will play in my mind forever—a luxury to listen to. The damp grass brings an earthy smell with it, and the air feels crisp and natural. How silly is it that something people are so bothered by can so easily soothe me? The rain makes me feel at home. It makes me feel like I am one with nature.

I can feel Miss Ladybug flutter away again.

Could her landing on me a second time be a greater sign of good luck?

I could only hope. The rain is still falling, but I decide to open my eyes and witness all the magic that it has to offer. I turn my head and I can't believe what I am seeing.

Are my eyes deceiving me, or am I really envisioning this?

There he is. Lying next to me, to my left.

I can't believe that he is here. How did he get here? He had to have snuck up next to me while my eyes were closed.

That handsome man. Look at him, soaking in all his glory, basking in his ethereal beauty, the rain hitting him in just the right places. A smile creeps up on my face, which makes his come out, those plump, soft lips guarding that bright white smile of his. It could make anyone's day better, no matter how sad they are.

His piercing green eyes burn into my pupils. The same green as the trees that surround us. Viridian, my favorite color in the entire world. His eyes, so big and bulging, I almost get worried sometimes that I'll get lost in them. Those eyes, stealing the spotlight from his gorgeous eyebrows. Those bushy monsters he always manages to tame and shape into a soft arch.

I swear, that jaw of his could cut diamonds. Not to mention, how perfect his nose is. Not too big, but not too small. Centered smack dab in the middle of his face, in line with the middle of his ears, which are pierced. His bouncing brown curls rest on the top of his head. The same color as my own hair. They fall to the side as he faces me, looking to his right.

I examine the rest of his body. His hands are being used as a pillow for his head. Without looking, I know he is wearing rings on those long fingers of his.

His legs stretch out way further than mine. After all, he is 6'3 and I am only 5'4. He looks so beautiful laying there with those sunflowers around him. There he is. The love of my life. Lying in this meadow with me while nature engulfs us, the rain still falling—our favorite thing. I cannot help but think of the ladybug. It was her who brought this luck to me. It was her I surely have to thank for this. Mine. Nature, my lover; all mine. In this moment together, forever. Everything we've ever hoped and dreamed of. Simply, our little perfection. What could possibly go wrong?

"Forrester," I reach out to him.

"Ivy, my love," he grabs my hand, entangling it in his.

"What are you doing here?" I question with a light heart.

"I came to visit you. A sun shower out in nature; I couldn't miss our favorite thing," he smiles.

Oh, that smile. My heart feels like it's melting. I could not be more in love with him than I am at this moment right now. My Forrester. My love, visiting me because he knows we have to be together for our favorite thing. Everything is perfect. The way the rain is hitting his face ever so lightly. The way his eyes are sparkling from the sunlight. How his brown curls are now damp and hanging. It is perfect. He is perfect.

"Come dance with me, baby," he speaks with a faint voice.

I can't help to control my smile. Dancing in the rain. He really *is* a romantic.

Forrester gets up without ever letting go of my hand and manages to get me up in the same motion. In the next movement, he wraps his other hand around the small of my back and we begin to twist and twirl all over the wet sunflowers.

"I've missed you, Ivy," he whispers into my ear.

"How could you have? We were just together this morning," I laugh.

"Just stay in this moment with me forever. You promise?"

He sounds serious.

"I promise, my love. Forever," I reassure him.

We continue to waltz in the meadow, rain still hitting our bodies. I take my hand and push through his dripping curls. How could this get any better? It is simply impossible. I smile at him again, and this time, Forrester smiles so big and so bright, it's more powerful than the sun. He untangles his hand from mine and gently places it onto my face. He glides his fingers across my face, caressing it as he makes his way towards my ear. He lightly moves my long brown hair, revealing my cheek.

Forrester is gazing directly into my eyes now. All I see is a pool of green. It's so mesmerizing. I can almost feel my eyes twinkle with love.

"I love you, Ivy," he gushes.

"I love you more," I demand.

I look up to see the sun shining ever so brightly, and millions of tiny droplets come down directly in my line of vision. I shut my eyes, allowing myself to subconsciously flow while dancing.

Suddenly, something soft brushes my lips. It's Forrester. I smile into his lips as he gently kisses me.

"It feels like forever since our last kiss," he says.

He's right. It does kind of feel like forever since our last kiss. I could have sworn I kissed him goodbye earlier this morning when we were leaving each other, I think, but I shrug it off.

"That's only because we miss each other so much when we're apart," I smile as I watch a smile grow on his face, too.

"You're right. I don't know what I would ever do without you," he kisses me again.

I could feel the rain start to get lighter and the sun brighter. We continue to dance on.

Nothing can stop us now.

He twirls me around into himself so that my back is to his chest. We sway like this for a while as he whispers sweet nothings into my ear. He spins me out and twists me around so that we are facing each other again. I rest my head on his shoulder as he rests his on my neck.

"I never want this moment to end," I whisper.

"Shh, it doesn't have to. As long as the rain keeps coming, we'll be together," he hushes me.

I freeze. *What does that mean?* I look back up at the sky, concerned now. I can see the clouds start to drift away.

The rain is slowly going away, but it has to keep coming! Forrester said so.

I look back at him. His perfect little nose centered in the line with the middle of his ears. Those piercing viridian eyes of his that I can't help but get lost in. That bright white smile of his underneath those soft lips. His gorgeous bushy eyebrows and the jaw that could cut diamonds.

Three drops, two drops, one. The rain is now gone. His damp curls are back to their bouncing brown state. His long fingers are slowly losing their grasp from mine. He is disappearing. But how? I watch as his tall legs become short, disappearing first as the rest of his body starts to look transparent. Suddenly, he is gone, vanished into thin air.

This can't be happening. I rub my eyes. *I must be seeing things.*

I open them and see nothing but green and blue surrounding me. I rub them again. Harder this time. Still nothing. Just fuzziness from the aggression.

He really is gone. My love. My everything. Gone.

I shake my head and my body, trying to shake the whole thing off.

Was he ever even here? Did I fall asleep in the grass and just suddenly awake when the rain stopped? What is happening to me?

I decide to gather myself together. No point in crying over spilled milk.

Maybe that ladybug wasn't so lucky after all. Was there even a ladybug?

I shake my head.

No, there had to be. Come on, Ivy. Get it together.

I take a deep breath and check my surroundings. Woods, every which way. Odd. I decide to make a right and walk in that direction. No harm in randomly choosing which way to go, I hope.

On my walk over to the woods, I spot a butterfly. *These must mean good luck or that an angel is watching over me.* I make the executive decision to follow it. The butterfly has to know where it's going better than I do. It's extremely beautiful, yellow and green. Not just any green, either. Viridian. I chuckle. Forrester has to be playing a game on me. So, I let it lead the way.

Mister Butterfly and I pick up a friend along the way. A snake. Viridian as well. The snake is doing a good job at keeping up with us, but snakes do slither rather quickly. We finally make it out of the meadow and into normal grass. The woods are just a few feet away from us. I can see an owl sitting on a branch in the first tree to the left. It's mesmerizing. Her bright, big viridian eyes. Again! Another animal who has the color viridian somewhere on them.

This has to be a joke. I have to be dreaming. I stop in my tracks and try to pinch myself back to reality. Except, it doesn't work. So, I try again. Nothing. I guess I really am awake. That's suspiciously odd. I take another foot forward and land on a branch, cracking it in half. I spot a deer dash out from behind a tree and start to run. A few seconds later, it is joined by three other friends chasing after it. I smile. Animals are adorable. They are just like us. They can sense pain, they can feel love, and they know who their friends and family are.

In the distance, I hear a ribbit, followed by another one a second later, almost like the frogs are taunting each other. I laugh and continue my journey. I look around as I walk. It's beautiful. Being surrounded by numerous tall trees with picture perfect green leaves sprouting from the branches. It's like a dream. Being in nature feels heavenly. Everywhere you look it's aesthetically pleasing. *Natural art*, as I like to call it. Every sound, unique. No two species alike. I wonder what animals think of humans when they see us. I bet they find us even more crazy than what we think when we see them. It's a weird world we live in.

In the trees above are flocks of birds, each having their own branch to call home. Blue, red, yellow. All types of colors and sizes. Taking a deep breath, the smell of pine cones and cedar fill the air. I get hit with an after scent of damp moss from the sun shower. All around are sounds of insects rattling, birds chirping, and branches cracking and popping. The most beautiful sounds in the world. This is what home is to me. I just wish Forrester was here to experience this loveliness with me. I sigh and decide to take a seat on a fallen branch.

My animal friends have gone away and I am left by myself again. Alone, feeling lonely this time around. I can't help but wonder if I am simply imagining all of this. For my sanity, I hope I am not. I love Forrester and I know he loves me. I had to have been dreaming when I imagined us dancing together in the rain. What a shame. That was the best moment we have shared together in a long time. I keep imagining his soft hands guiding my back as we danced. His feet leading mine as we turned. His smile burning the same one onto my face. That kiss.

A single tear drops from my eye and I quickly wipe it away. This is foolish of me. I'll see Forrester again when I go home. Right now, I need only to enjoy the time I have in nature.

I place my body weight onto one foot first and then the other.

No point in sitting in the middle of the woods sulking.

I continue on my journey through the forest. As I walk, I can hear water running in the background. It almost sounds like a river stream somewhere far away. I decide to let the sound guide me to where it is.

Rain isn't the same thing as a river, but water is water, right?

If Forrester said we would be together as long as the rain was still falling, there shouldn't be a reason why we couldn't be together if there was water flowing somewhere. *Or so I hope.*

This idea makes me happy again. I might be able to see him and actually be with him if I have the chance. *God, I hope I get the chance.* I am determined now to find this river. I can hear it roaring louder in my right ear, so I decide to go in that direction.

As I make my way through, I see a fox standing in my pathway. Most people would run in the other direction. However, I am not afraid, or like most people. Yes, they only come out at night in search of food, alone, but this one seems different though. It seems lonely, like me.

The fox is beautiful. His reddish-brown fur is shining in the sunlight that makes its way down through the trees;

almost like a spotlight. The white on its chest and tail stand out the most. Kind of like Forrester's teeth when he smiles.

Man, I miss that smile. The fox seems to not mind my presence either. He turns to the right and starts walking in the direction of the water. *Smart fox.* I follow him. What harm could it bring? I make sure to keep my distance, so the fox doesn't feel threatened. We make a good team. With each step we take, the sound grows closer. I can now hear how fast the water flow is. It must be cool to the touch, something I need on this hot summer day. The fox turns a bend and then disappears. *What is it with everything disappearing on me today?* I shake my head and turn the bend as well.

There it is. The river. Not long in width, but extremely long in length. It probably goes on for miles. I wonder where it could lead to. Suddenly, I am drawn to follow the flow of the water. I can see it is heading west. I walk along the grass next to it so that I don't accidentally fall in. I can see fish racing their way through the stream. Lily pads resting where the stream doesn't hit. Frogs sitting on top, minding their own business. One or two of them catching flies with their long tongues. Nature truly is amazing. To my right I hear a branch break. Like something stepped on it. I stop in my tracks and I turn to look. Not something, but someone. *Could it be? Is it really him this time?*

"Forrester!" I shout.

"Ivy, my love," he smiles.

"You've found me, huh?" he laughs.

"I've been looking all over for you!" I yell, annoyed that he is laughing.

"How did you do that?" I demand.

"Do what?"

"Don't play dumb with me. You vanished. Into thin air. I want to know how you did that!"

"Please, my love. Don't be angry with me," he says, a sadness in his tone. "Cross the river and we can be together, forever. Just like you promised."

"Together, forever. Just like you promised." That has a nice ring to it.

I do what he says and I take my first step down towards the river. It looks scary once I'm standing in front of it and much wider than I thought it was. I take a deep breath. *If this is what it takes for us to be together, then so be it.* I find my first rock that looks suitable enough to step on, but it only fits one foot. I take a big step forward and leap onto the rock. I try to catch my balance. I'm not that coordinated. Once I feel confident enough standing on the tiny rock, I search for my next step forward. The next one is bigger. Big enough to fit both feet on it, at least. With my left foot, I take another step, my right foot quickly catching up.

I look around now in search of rocks, but the next one is a distance away. There is no way I will be able to make it with the stream flowing this fast.

"Forrester," I yell.

"I can't go any farther. Come and meet me," I practically beg.

"I can't cross the river, my love. You just have to trust me on this one," he yells back with a soothing voice.

I start to panic. If he can't cross the river, how am I ever going to make it over to him? I close my eyes and take a deep breath. *Think, Ivy. All you need to do is think.* I turn to my left and I spot a big branch. One that looks sturdy and thick enough for my feet to cross over. I lay it down so that it is resting on the edge of the rock I am standing on, and the rock I need to get to.

"You can do this, baby," Forrester reassures me.

I shake my head in agreement and I place my right foot onto the branch. I test my balance and it seems like it can hold me. I walk slow and steadily across the branch until I make it over. Once I am safe on the rock, I let out a sigh of relief.

This time when I look up, Forrester seems farther away from me. *How could that be?* I am getting closer, but he is getting farther. *That doesn't make any sense.* I try my hardest to make it across the river as quickly as I can so that it stops growing in distance. I am out of luck. With every step I take, it seems as if Forrester is getting further away from me.

"Hold out your hand," he yells.

I stretch my hand out as far as I possibly can while he does the same. I am struggling to reach him. I can feel myself falling as I stretch out farther. As I fall, Forrester's hand is in a direct line with mine. However, when my hand reaches for his, he slips away from me. I watch as my hand falls right through his. I look up at him as he is vanishing into thin air again.

I close my eyes as I start crying and screaming on my fall down into the stream. This time, I can feel someone shaking me. As I come to, I can see doctors and nurses surrounding me by the dozen. A flatline noise in the background settles back into a normal, but fast heart rate.

"This can't be happening. Please tell me this isn't happening," I yell, struggling to get out of the hospital bed.

"I'm very sorry, Ivy," a doctor says, trying to calm me down as a nurse brings me over ice water.

"You were in a terrible car accident this morning with your boyfriend," he continues. "I regret to inform you that he did not make it."

Suddenly, my whole world freezes.

LOE POOL

BY

TERRY LANDER

The smash of a fourth plate shot up the stairs and into

Henry's room where he was covering his ears, both hands merging with the dark brown hair he'd inherited from his mother, Helen. His eyes were tightly shut as he hid behind a huge box of Lego, his favourite stuffed toys on top, guarding the door to his room.

His parents often fought. Although, this time, it was much worse. His mother had found a receipt for flowers and chocolates in his father's discarded jeans as she'd gone to wash them and figured that he must have been unfaithful since they hadn't appeared. Since Henry was only eight years old, he didn't realise the extent of what was happening beneath him as Helen started to aggressively kick the sofa and curse her husband's name before pulling open a can of beer.

He had shrugged her mood off earlier, but when his father came home, he'd witnessed crockery flying urgently across the room and had run upstairs to cower into his present position. He'd stayed here for over an hour.

Henry felt he had to leave the atmosphere of the house, which seemed to be closing in on him. He was certain that his parents would never hurt him, yet also felt that he would rather be in a more pleasant place on such a beautiful day. The sun had streamed through his bedroom window as he'd thrown the curtains open that morning and he'd smiled as its warmth radiated across his skin.

As the argument developed, he thought about how enticing the light had been and decided to slip out of the back door of the house. To do this, he had to carefully tiptoe down the stairs and move into the kitchen, past the raging argument that seemed unlikely to conclude any time soon. From there, he could crack the back door gently and slide out, a short walk through his garden leading him to the road outside. With his plan in place, he removed his hands from his ears, opened his eyes and stood up, the noise as prominent as it had been when he'd first hidden.

Moving past his parents was meant to be the difficult part of the journey, yet Henry found that neither could take their eyes off the other for the short time that he was in the room. Instead of gentle steps, he could well have danced across the living room and still made it out. He sighed as he reached the back door and opened it, maintaining a quieter exit as he knew his escape was important. *How I spent the rest of the day was going to be in my control,* he thought.

The curb at the edge of the quiet thoroughfare offered ample protection as Henry made his way towards Penrose, a wooded area that his mother often took him to when he needed to release excess energy. He felt the heat of the sun as he walked, removing his green jumper and tying it around his waist. The robot that had adorned his chest now faced his back and was replaced with a Lego dinosaur on an orange T-shirt.

There were unusually few people or cars around for it being the afternoon, but Henry hadn't noticed as he meandered along the path, the tension leaving his body more with every step. He was starting to develop a migraine while in his room, the final remnants of which completely left him as he saw the entrance to Penrose appearing in front of him.

The granite posts holding the fence stood proudly as they guarded the wide path, forbidding vehicles to enter the pedestrian walkway. Henry made his way onto the path through a small gap beside the fence, which opened out to show the black tarmac, the depth of the fresh material swallowing the shadows of the trees on both sides. To his left, a gentle stream flowed away and carried the discarded leaves to Loe Pool just two miles away.

Henry followed his mother to Penrose at least once a week, although they rarely walked for long enough to see Loe Pool. On the rare occasions that they did, Henry was warned never to swim in the lake. He'd heard the tale of the curse, how every seven years a new soul was lost to the infamous waters. As he'd heard the words, he looked over the placid lake with its tiny ripples and inviting coolness, only to wonder what exactly made the lake so dangerous. Ducks and swans were regular visitors to Loe Pool and they were able to cruise along the surface without any issues, leading him to sport a quizzical look. Perhaps, there was something under the water, a beast or a massive fish, that pulled unwitting visitors to their watery grave. He didn't want to think about such a creature, yet the potential was burned into his mind and reappeared every time he heard the name of Loe Pool.

Today, the walk had been so easy and calming that it was almost inevitable for him to end up at the lake. Two dog walkers were the only people to see him, both of whom looked in his direction, but didn't give him a second glance. Henry figured that his radiant smile must have given them the confidence that he should have been there alone, and this made him smile wider, the independence suggested by the encounters cheering him up. By the time he could see the dark waters of the lake, he was almost strutting along.

Loe Pool was a very unusual freshwater feature. Separated from the sea by a mere quarter of a mile of sand, it overlooked a tempting beach that could have seen families enjoying the surf on one side of the bar and gentle swimming in the stillness of the lake. However, signs around the area prohibited entry into either stretch of water due to the high, unseen currents that would quickly drag a bather into trouble. Henry's mother had never mentioned the currents, concentrating instead on the curse that was written into the mythology of the surrounding towns. Henry thought about how much he might struggle when he first saw the water, although he was pleased to be present in the still air.

During their visits, Helen and Henry often played games together that school friends partook of in the playground, such as Tag and Bulldog. Their games always required more than one player and so he looked around for something to occupy him, finding a pinecone and branch that had fallen from a nearby tree. He threw the pinecone into the air and watched as it dropped, hoping to catch it with the branch as he swung it like a bat. However, it descended too quickly, striking Henry on the head, causing a small bump under his hair. He rubbed the sore spot and closed his eyes, the pain not enough to concern him, yet certainly unavoidably there.

"That was silly," came a voice from nearby.

Henry opened his eyes in an instant, the sound seeming strangely familiar. He thought about what had been said and frowned.

"I didn't do it on purpose," he replied with annoyance in his voice.

He squinted to catch sight of the visitor, noticing that it was a girl about his age.

"It really hurt."

The girl laughed quaintly, still walking towards Henry. "Aw, you poor thing."

Henry couldn't tell if she was being sarcastic, so he kept quiet and let her speak once more. The pain subsided, although he didn't notice as his full attention was on the girl.

"Why are you here alone?"

A huffing noise emanated from Henry's nose before he responded.

"I could ask you the same thing. Who are you?"

Giggling, the girl smiled widely and held out a well-tanned hand that contrasted sharply with her bright, pink dress.

"I'm Gracie. I'm here on my own because my parents let me, so long as I don't talk to strangers. How about you?"

Still squinting, more out of curiosity by this point, Henry shook Gracie's hand.

"I'm a stranger," he said sharply.

"Are you?" Gracie asked with a smirk.

Henry frowned at her reply.

"There's no way your parents just let you out like this. I snuck out because my parents are always arguing, and now they've started throwing plates."

He thought about the argument and sighed.

Calming down, he continued, "I wanted to be somewhere quiet, so I came here."

The still air picked up very briefly as they finished their handshake, a breeze invading the area uninvited and leaving as quickly as it arrived. Gracie looked down towards the floor as her wavy, blonde hair recovered from the draught.

"My parents argue, too. It seems we have a lot in common."

The revelation hit Henry firmly as he noticed a sadness pass over Gracie's features. He smiled for the first time since their meeting, forcing it to show that he cared.

"Let's play together and forget our parents, then," he said with enthusiasm, picking up the stick that he'd thrown after being hit by the pinecone.

"It's a good idea, but I have a better one." Gracie took Henry by the hand and took him into a clearing by the trees, selecting a long, straight stick that had little in the way of bark and offshoots. "Find yourself a stick that looks like this one."

Peering around on the floor, Henry excitedly searched for an identical stick. He managed to find one that was very similar, although he didn't realise that it was a long time dead. The two of them attached vines from a nearby bush to make very crude bows, which they coupled with smaller, sharper sticks. Finally, they made their way to a wide based tree for target practice.

"I used to do this with my mum all the time," Gracie proclaimed as she lined up her first arrow.

Her technique was exquisite and it reminded Henry of the Robin Hood film he'd seen the previous month. Gracie was perfectly motionless until she let the vine go, the two of them watching as the arrow flew effortlessly through the air and into the side of the tree.

"Now it's your turn."

Stepping onto the same spot that Gracie had shot from, Henry lined himself up in relation to the tree. He stood firm, holding the bow in his left hand and grabbing the vine and arrow in his right. As he went to pull the vine back, the dry stick gave way and snapped towards the top, the cracking sound making Henry jump.

The arrow dropped harmlessly onto the floor while the bow snapped out of his hand and jumped into the air, landing nearby a few seconds later.

Watching the spectacle closely, Gracie burst into uncontrollable laughter.

"You're not very good at sports, are you?" she hollered between bouts of chuckles.

As her laughter subsided, she could see that Henry was quite hurt by the suggestion.

"Aw, it's alright. Everybody's good at something. Try this."

As she spoke, Gracie took a large branch that had long fallen and placed some dry grass on the top.

"What are you doing with that?" Henry asked, his voice filled with caution.

There were few options at this stage, although he hoped perhaps Gracie was making a wooden doll, but starting in the centre.

Looking up at him, Gracie chuckled. "I've done this a thousand times before, don't worry. You just have to be careful to put it out before it gets too big."

Henry had seen many documentaries warning of the dangers of fire, though Gracie made him feel somehow safe. He figured it must have been her previous experience that calmed him slightly, and so he watched in awe as sparks created a small flame inside the grass. A few short blows later and the flames started to rise, after which Gracie picked up the sides of the stick and walked them to the side of the river. Without flinching, she placed the branch into the lake to extinguish the flame.

"Your turn," she offered with a smile.

The discarded branch started to float off as Henry battled with himself. He didn't really want to try, the flames themselves being beautifully constructed under Gracie's expert gaze. He also wanted to make up for the poor show with the bow and arrow, which seemed to casually win in his mind. He found a similarly shaped branch and copied Gracie exactly, although his movement with the stick in his hand was too slow to create the necessary friction. Gracie guided him with her voice, yet fifteen solid minutes of trying got the better of Henry.

"My hands hurt. This is daft," he said in frustration.

Gracie chuckled softly, her face kind as she congratulated him on his efforts.

"I bet there's something you're really good at. Can you swim?"

The words cut through the air more sharply than Gracie's arrow had. Henry froze on the spot, looking first towards the sea and then at the lake, both of which he'd been forbidden to enter. He thought about the creature, the undiscovered Loe Pool monster that lured people to their deaths, wondering if he would be its next victim.

"Not really..." he offered quietly, hoping Gracie would think of something else for them to do.

Unfortunately, she didn't.

"You'll be great. Everyone can swim. I've seen babies swim," she said casually, turning towards the lake.

"I'm not really supposed to," Henry replied, hoping he wouldn't have to plead with her.

He watched as she turned around and raised an eyebrow.

"Who's going to stop you?" Gracie spoke deliberately, her tone goading him with every word.

Her smile widened before she turned once more, her exaggerated walk towards the lake both confident and deliberate. Checkmate.

In an instant, Henry thought of a thousand other reasons why he couldn't go swimming, including having no costume and needing armbands. Gracie seemed unwilling to argue and so he followed on slowly, deciding to take things one step at a time. He'd take his clothes off, inch by inch, until he was down to his underwear. Then, he'd slowly slide into the lake and take a look for the beast, darting out of the water the second he saw it.

By the time he made it to the water's edge, Gracie was already in.

"It's so beautiful around here and this water really cools you down," Gracie offered as she continued to tread water.

She then swam across the lake, moving slightly to the left with each stroke until she completed a full circle and stopped in front of Henry.

"Come on!" she laughed.

His heart was beating as he studied the murky water, a voice clear within his head. He knew not to go in, his mother telling him just that, her words repeating the details of the curse.

However, as with the arrow and the fire, Gracie had shown him the way. If she was swimming without concern in the lake, then maybe Helen had been wrong about the whole thing. It wasn't like she'd been in herself to confirm the presence of such a curse.

Taking a deep breath, the young lad stepped into the ripples Gracie had just made and slid down the bank, ducking his head under the water to acclimatise to the temperature. As he returned to the surface, he could feel the sun beating down on him once more and appreciated the chill of the water on his skin. More importantly, there was no sign of any wildlife other than the birds that he was used to seeing.

"See? You nearly missed out on this because your parents told you not to, and they're not even here!" she almost sang, laughing heartily once more.

Chuckling along, Henry started to swim in circles around Gracie, figuring that laps to the other side of the lake may leave him tired and unable to get back.

"This was a good idea," he said in submission, finally having fun.

He looked towards his new friend, deciding in the moment to splash her with a giant wave created by his two hands. Gracie laughed and reciprocated, the noise seemingly unheard by anybody who may have been passing.

Half an hour later, and with his stomach rumbling, Henry decided that he was too tired to continue swimming. Gracie called him a chicken with a beaming grin, then watched as he departed the water and sat on the side for a few moments. The warm air dried him slightly, but it was never going to be enough to remove every drop from his sodden clothes, so he pulled on his outerwear and put the dampness out of his mind.

"I think I have to go home," he told Gracie, surprised that she hadn't emerged behind him.

"Sure," she said, a further surprise to Henry.

"See you again soon, new friend," she continued before swimming away from him, almost fading into the distance.

He frowned at her actions as he'd hoped they would at least walk out of the park together. At that point, he realised that Gracie had been there when he'd arrived and could well have come from the other direction. He shrugged, turning to make his way home, his emotional day ending on a high.

The walk home began innocently enough, another dog walker present on the path. Henry continued to look past her towards the end of the trail when her spaniel started to growl, baring teeth in Henry's direction. His eyes widened, still set on their original target, and the dog barked viciously towards him. The owner shouted the dog's name with a confused expression, moving towards them both to retrieve her mischievous pup.

"What's gotten into you, hey?" she asked, her face contracted in puzzlement.

Henry picked up his pace, no longer feeling the warmth of the air around him.

The largest town surrounding Penrose was well populated, with most of Henry's family living nearby. His mother and her brother had been brought up in the town and he regularly saw his favourite uncle driving past in a restored 1980's Ford Escort. Henry loving the sharp, edgy bodywork. He recognised the car whenever he saw it in an instant, the off-white colour appearing dull in comparison to other vehicles around it. As he approached the gate and turned towards his house, the car made an appearance in the distance and he immediately shifted from the nervousness caused by the dog to the excitement at seeing his uncle.

Two other cars passed Henry before the Escort and he patiently waited for his chance to wave, noticing that his uncle seemed preoccupied with the radio as he kept looking down towards it.

Henry expected at least a short wave as he passed, but his uncle clearly hadn't noticed him as he pulled up level and then sped into the distance. Henry's arm was feverishly gesturing, but his face dropped as he realised that it would not be returned. Dejected, he started the short walk back to his house, adamant he'd tell his mother in the hope that his uncle would be made to apologise.

As it was, the incident was forgotten by the time Henry made it to his front door. Memories of his parents' argument filled his mind as he wondered what kind of mood they'd be in, his unexplained absence surely adding to their potential rage. He paused at the end of the garden, taking a deep breath before he crossed into the house. All was silent as the door swung inwards, the remnants of crockery still littering the kitchen floor.

"Mum?" The single word crept through the house with a cautious tone.

He walked slowly into the kitchen, closing the door with less finesse than he'd opened it and causing it to clunk into the frame. The noise clearly roused Helen as she appeared in an instant in front of him from the living room.

"Henry, where on Earth have you been?" Her eyes were as wide as her mouth while quick movements confirmed that she was not in a pleasant mood.

Henry dropped his face, placing his hands behind his back in an act of submission.

"I went to Penrose. I got really scared about your fight."

The declaration hit Helen and her panic turned to sorrow as she moved forward, embracing him as she did so.

"I'm sorry, sweetheart, we weren't mad at you. We were… it's over now, I promise. Why are you wet?"

The question made his nerves heighten once more as he realised that he had a confession to make. He'd hoped the warm air would take enough of the moisture from his body that he wouldn't be found out, but now that he had, his words were surely critical.

"I met a girl at Penrose. She told me that she'd been swimming in Loe Pool before and said that it was fine."

"What girl, Henry?" Helen asked with a frown.

He squinted and looked to the left, trying to remember exactly what she looked like.

"Her name was Gracie. She had a pink dress and curly hair. She was very funny and taught me to…" Henry tailed off as Helen looked at him in horror, the description hitting her like nothing he'd ever said before.

His fear of telling her about the swimming was nothing compared to the view of his mother's contorted features.

"Take me there, right now please."

The urgency in her voice was horrifying and confusing as he wondered if his punishment awaited him at the end of the long walk. Nevertheless, he obediently turned and walked back out of the door, leading Helen by the hand.

The actions of Henry's uncle were briefly remembered as he saw the gate for the third time that day, although he

was never going to interrupt the awkwardness with a simple
tale of how he'd been unusually missed by a favoured family
member.

There were still very few people using the walkway to
the lake as they strolled quickly along it, the sun starting to
drop in the distance. Leaves cascaded from the trees in
spirals, landing on the ground and remaining still until they
were walked past or over, the shuffling feet causing the
disturbance.

A squirrel looked on from the safety of a wall, the tall
grass on top hiding its features from the trespassers. It had
been successfully gathering nuts, blissfully ignorant of those
who passed during the day. However, the hurried footsteps of
the two approaching humans caused it to watch vigilantly,
making no sound or movement until they had long passed. It
then went back to make a final collection, relieved that their
urgent actions were not likely to cause issues in its direct
vicinity.

Helen had started crying as they'd entered Penrose and
Henry felt like he was in for a world of punishment, keeping
his eyes fixed forward to delay the seemingly inevitable.
Neither said a word to each other until they were nearly there
when Helen finally broke the silence.

"Please tell me this isn't goodbye," she said through
sobs, her voice breaking Henry's heart as it landed.

"What do you mean, Mum?" he asked.

The sunlight broke into an orange haze as the lake came
into view, the ripples becoming more visible with every step.
The dog walker with the spaniel stood by the edge, the dog
obediently by the side of its master. Both were calm as they
perused the scene, Helen shaking her head as she watched
them.

"Why did you go swimming in the lake, Henry? Please be honest, I won't be cross."

Emergency vehicles came into view now, their lights flashing as the occupants spoke and shook their heads. Henry looked up at his mother with pleading eyes, knowing he had to tell the truth.

"I'm sorry. Gracie said it would be alright."

Henry's mother tried to swallow the lump in her throat, speaking to Henry for the final time when she knew she could not succeed.

"When you were very young, you had a sister. One day, she went missing and we couldn't find her. There was a big search, everyone got involved, but there was no sign of her. I'd warned her about the curse of Loe Pool. I even took her down as I did with you when you were young to show her where she must never go swimming. I knew in my heart that she was there. Gracie loved the lake as much as you did, but I didn't want to think that we would never see her again. I know what's coming next."

Helen looked down to see that Henry had gone, the light from the sun intensifying slowly until it almost blinded those in the area. The emergency service personnel shielded their eyes, audibly gasping as the flash came and finally subsided at the same rate.

A police officer was guarding the cordon and advised Helen not to go near the scene, giving as few details as he dared. Seeing how distraught she was, he asked if he could help and Helen simply shook her head, looking across to the lake.

Her ability to speak had ceased with the flash of the sun. She simply mouthed, my son, and put her hand over her thundering heart.

The officer understood immediately, allowing her to move to the side of the lake where Henry was lying perfectly still.

The spaniel had been characteristically calm since finding his body, but started to sniff the air, a furrowed brow indicating that it was not content. It started to pick up a scent on the ground and guided its owner towards the side of the lake, dipping its head into the cool, still water. Suddenly it recoiled, darting backwards and whining in distress. The owner called another officer, who quickly responded by putting her hand into the lake.

While Henry had been removed from the water in a beautiful condition, the ragged pink dress adorning the second body was not for the faint hearted. Helen watched with her hand over her mouth as the officer pulled the body gently out and laid Gracie on the bank beside her brother.

One final breeze blew through the scene, but it was not the cause of shivering for those present. The gloomy waters followed the direction of the wind, tiny waves visible to those who wished to look away from the scene. The sun finally descended behind the horizon and plunged the woodland more quickly into darkness, the artificial lighting not enough to keep the exhausted animals awake for the night. As they retired, the trees continued to drop their leaves periodically, the cycle of the woods continuing unmoved.

The Huldra's Treasure

By

Dalila Fuentes

Deep within the woods filled with dark magical

entities that hide away from mankind, humans have staked their claim on the world, destroying everything in their path for riches, honor, and status. Most creatures are diverse in terms of good and evil. Some are kind and peaceful while others are hideous and cruel monsters. However, all of them have one thing in common. They are all protected by the beautiful Huldra who goes by the name Revna.

Revna walked with grace amongst the many creatures that reside in the Hallerbos woods. In her sanctuary, where she rests, is a pink pearl hidden from the eyes of men. For if men take it, then evil would flourish, but if the pearl is given, then the one who is gifted such a pearl may have an abundance of peace and good fortune—if Revna so chooses. But her heart is blackened due to the loss of her sisters.

Memories of several women frolicking in the woods with her flash before her. Sisters, singing and dancing, protecting the pearl as the creatures, animals, and the woods feel their happy spirit. Yet, their memory fades to red when Revna remembers their death. The pixies had gone out searching for each one and found bodies drained of blood and left in the open without a proper burial. The trees sway in the wind with anguish. They can feel the presence of someone entering their domain with malice. Revna whispers to the wind to carry a warning to the rest of the creatures and a cry for the darkness to prepare the trial for every human that dares enter their land.

On the other side of the woods, where the entrance is mostly hidden from the human eye, where some can bypass the illusion of poisonous flowers scattered throughout the trees, is a man with a scar on the right side of his face from his brow down to his jawbone. A fierce and mischievous look crosses his face as he is able to see past the magic that hides what he has been searching for. The man standing at the entrance is Ulf, an intelligent Viking with dirty blonde hair and eerie ghostlike blue eyes. Legends speak of people who are brown with ghostlike blue eyes. They say they are ones who can outrun magical beings and see the truth more than other humans.

Revna walks over to the window and reflects on her magical surroundings. She had always loved the peaceful Hallerbos forest with its iridescent, ancient bed of bluebells. It was a place that encouraged her to think more often, which had a tendency to make her feel sad. She could see through the eyes of her falcon, her familiar, who flew high in the sky. She could see he was not a regular human, which worried her the most. Revna gulped. She glanced at her own reflection, a fierce, vicious Huldra with brunette hair and green eyes that matched the forest.

Well then, let's see how you fare against my trials, human.

Revna turned to a tree stump that was hollow with clear crystal liquid showing her what she wanted to see or create through her dark magic. The swiftness of her fingers left a cloud of mist over the first area the man walked into.

At the entrance, Ulf made the first step to enter Revna's domain. As he walked, the mist engulfed his figure, making him disappear from the world, as if he was never there to begin with. As Ulf strolled deeper into the woods, he looked on either side of him, taking in the eerie beauty of the forest, bewitched by the animals that graze on the grassy ground.

Ulf listened closely to all the sounds: the cops of birds, the rustles of deers grazing grass, the trickle of water streams, and the howls of wolves. It all became silent when he stood before a large figure with its back towards him. Ulf took his sword out of his sheath, stepping slowly.

"Do you think you could take it?" an urgent tone came out of the large beast.

"I believe I may have a chance. Why?" Ulf smiled crookedly, swinging his sword in the air ready to strike the large being, unsure if it was a fae or a dark entity.

"Stupid boy, you have no idea who you stand before."

The creature slowly stood on its hind legs where it became apparent that it had an animalistic figure. Ulf's smile fell slightly when he saw the creature was Fenrir, a wolf-like, eagle-like being that was birthed by the mischievous god Loki and the giantess Angroboda.

"What is an ugly shite like you doing here in these woods?" boasted Ulf like a man who believed he could win.

This annoyed Fenrir to no end. In a blink of an eye, he rushed towards Ulf to swipe his talons against him. Ulf managed to get away just in time by falling down and rolling over away from him.

He took out his sword ready to strike at a moment's notice. Fenrir growled lowly, becoming increasingly annoyed by this man's persistence to keep going. Nevertheless, he pursued the human and a long-winded battle commenced between them. A few times, scratches and wounds were given just as fierce to match the opponent's strength. Over time, Ulf gave more damage to Fenrir than the beast initially thought. Something about his sword cut much deeper than any opponent's weapon he'd faced.

"Never in my life have I faced a weapon that could take me down, but you… I smell nothing that 's been blessed by a witch."

Ulf brought out his crooked smile again, swinging his sword in the air as if he'd already won. He took a small dagger and threw it behind his head striking a small animal to the ground. It was a falcon that fell from the tree, the little spy Revna had in case she wanted a closer look. From the other side of the forest, Revna gasped in slight pain and teared up with the thought of the death of her precious bird.

"That's it! I'm going to have your heart," Revna whispered into the ground where roots spread throughout the forest.

The roots glowed to her words and began to rush off through its network. Once the whisper reached Fenrir, he stopped his stance and accepted the command Revna had given.

"Who said I was only human?" Ulf said, not noticing Fenrir's different look.

Ulf charged toward Fenrir, leaping into the air with his sword in a strike position and cutting through to his heart. It took Ulf seconds to realize that Fenrir had surrendered to his fate, but once noticed, he felt disgusted with himself. He'd never fought an opponent who did not fight back.

"Wait, why would you surrender?"

Fenrir chuckled lightly, looking up to Ulf, giving him a look that said it would all be over soon. Without speaking a word, Fenrir turned into dust, nothing saying his presence had just died there.

Ulf cleaned his blade from any remains of Fenrir's being. He questioned why he would surrender, leaving him feeling like his victory was nothing more than a bloody accident. He continued the journey without another thought to the death of Fenrir.

It seemed he'd been walking for many miles, but he had no idea how close he was to Revna. Meanwhile, she'd been speaking to all of the living creatures to stay away from this human, saying he's more dangerous and very much perceptive of his surroundings. Many of the pixies kept tabs on the human man who walked with a dangerous aura, informing Revna of every step he took.

Okay, human. Keep going. You're mine soon.

As Ulf continued his journey, he reached an area that felt off. The air felt like it disappeared every time he tried to breathe. He looked for a sign of any presence, but it was not until it came out of the shadows that he could sense what it was.

"Oi, you can go ahead," said the being. This surprised Ulf, but he stayed to have a chat and try to understand the world that he entered.

"Maybe you can tell me why you won't fight, dwarf."

"You are not my war. However, count the breaths you take for they will be the last. You will wish you never entered our domain."

Ulf chuckled at his warning. The confidence was astounding to him.

"I killed your fiercest warrior and you tell me I should still be scared? I think you are mistaken."

The dwarf spoke nothing more. Instead, he merely watched the human, studying him, understanding what he got out of stealing from them. Without another word, the dwarf disappeared into the shadows, leaving no trace that he had been there speaking to Ulf.

Ulf walked on, continuing the journey, not understanding just yet why the second trial never fought him. As he continued his stroll through the forest, it took a moment for him to notice its details, listening closely to what was nearby, hearing the small whispers from tiny creatures, the cries from other animals, and looking towards the sky where many birds seemed to gather, looking like spectators, vultures, waiting for him to die so they can feast on his flesh.

Ulf reached an area where the sound of a fiddle was being played. The melody mimicked the wind and the lake, creating a dance for any creature to frolic in.

It was a fossegrimen, or grim for short. They were not very violent creatures, but would take any offer, even though a goat's head with intricate details was preferred. The grim was sitting on a small patch of land in the middle of a lake that glowed green. Small pixies danced to his tune, whispering like bells.

"Yes, my pretties, dance, dance! Hahaha."

"Excuse me. I don't mean to interrupt your merrymaking, but can you tell me where I can find the Huldra?"

The word Huldra stopped the grim from playing his music. It began to breathe heavily, slightly crouching to his shoulders. It stood to his small height with a lanky body, wet mossy hair, and scaling green flesh. It turned around giving Ulf a stink eye.

"No!"

"No?"

"How dare you stop my playing! As you can see, the pixies are in need of relaxation. They are stressed beyond belief and I must help them relax! Leave now! Leave!"

The small bell-like whispers from the pixies begin to shake their small frail bodies.

There wasn't much Ulf could do. The grim continued to play his tune on the fiddle, dancing with the pixies, Ulf forgotten from their minds as if he'd never stopped the music.

Ulf continued to tread across the forest thinking how much further he had to walk. The day was turning into nightfall, and soon, everything would no longer look

magical. Fog began to descend to the ground, slowly
blocking his view from where he felt he had to go.

He realized he was not alone in this forest, hearing a
heavy breath close by. He took his sword out to fight
whatever was next, but any time he thought it was close, it
seemed to change positions as if taunting him.

A sound of a bite near his ear caught him off guard. Ulf
turned and swung his sword, but missed the strike. The
taunting continued, almost as if planned to make Ulf so tired
he could no longer hold his own weapon.

Before he could take another swing, a humming sound
distracted him. He turned trying to locate where it was
coming from and it was as if the fog knew what he wanted.
It dissipated, giving him a clear view of a brightly lit area
that had tall trees.

The entrance, Ulf thought.

He walked further inside to investigate the sound. The
light showed through flowers and leaves that seemed to glow
in the presence of a womanly figure. As he walked further,
he saw a woman with dark long brown hair and a tail. She
began to sing an old song he had not heard in a while, a song
where pain and suffering are part of life.

The woman turned around in all of her naked glory, and
Ulf couldn't help but eye the woman, despite knowing it was
anything but a woman. Still, he hawked at her, taking in the
illusion of this creature. Revna smirked, the pixies flying all
around her whispering the tales they witnessed with this
human man. She laughed despite anger still boiling for his
daring killing of her beautiful falcon.

"I know you might be wondering why you only faced
one of my trials. In truth, it's because you killed what was
mine."

He could not grasp what she meant until remembering that he had killed a falcon for his suspicions that he was being watched.

"Sorry, love. Didn't know I had killed your pet. Nevertheless, it's not polite to watch someone like some creeper."

Revna rolled her eyes and began to circle him with a fierce glint, she watched him closely trying to analyze what he might do to her. She has enough knowledge on how he fights others, changing his moves according to whom he's against.

"Why do you want it?"

"Excuse me?"

"Why do you want it?"

It didn't take long for Ulf to understand the question. He gave her a mischievous grin that said, does it matter?

"I don't think you should have it," Revna looked Ulf dead in the eyes.

The silence between them was unbearable until, finally, Revna laughed in a maniacal way.

"Oh, you are so confident enough to think you could take it from me?"

Ulf couldn't understand what her deal was yet, but it didn't deter him from what he wanted. However, he didn't know that what he desired could destroy the very essence of woods and Revna would rather die than let a human take what belonged to her and what kept everyone alive.

"You believe what I have is simply treasure. Yes, it's a beautiful pearl, but taking it is not without its consequences—consequences you can't even fathom."

Revna pointed to the pearl that glistened underneath the moonlit sky. There were vines attached to it that glowed an iridescent green. The same thing he saw back in the woods.

Despite realizing the truth of the pearl, human greed overpowered his connection to nature.

"Sorry, but I don't give a damn. I want it. It will be mine whether you like it or not."

"Well then, let's do this."

Before Ulf could understand what would happen next, Revna rushed towards him with long talons, taking a good swipe to his chest. The wounds weren't deep enough to stop him from fighting, but it still made him hurt.

"Bloody hell!"

Ulf unsheathed his sword, taking a defensive stance to fight back. Revna swung her arms as fast and hard as she could. Ulf could block each blow, but they were still strong enough to push him to the edge. Repeated attacks and not letting up, he realized she was trying to tire him out. He decided on a different approach and fell to the ground before she could give him another hit. Ulf rolled over behind her and slashed her back with one swipe. The cut made her scream in agony, and she realized it was embedded in powerful steel, but there was something else, something stronger that was able to take down Fenrir.

He swung again and she leapt onto the trees. Exhausted, she tried to take a moment to think, but Ulf wouldn't let her rest. He took out his bow and arrow and shot at her, missing, but she could see the steel burning the wood on her right. She gasped in fright, realizing she may lose and everyone else in the woods who depended on her would cease to exist.

Ulf could see the terror in her eyes, gleeing in delight. He shot again, but each shot missed as she continued to leap, climbing up the trees. Ulf stopped, steadying his breath. With one eye, he focused his energy into getting her. The next jump Revna took, he let go of the air he held in and the arrow shot her ankle.

The steel stung in her flesh, not enough to kill her but enough to make her weak and unable to run. She fell from her trees all the way to the ground, the sound of bells chiming in the air as they feared the loss of their protector. All of them dispersed in fright, not willing to watch the final blow to the beautiful Huldra.

As she laid on the ground unconscious, Ulf walked slowly to the beautiful creature, eyeing her body, her dark flowing hair, the sharpness of her talons.

She's dead. Now, no one can stop me from taking the pearl, Ulf thought.

He stood over her body, taking out a hand knife. He crouched down to whisper in her ear. Even though he knew she couldn't hear him, he decided to tell her what was in the steel.

"I could see in your eyes you were wondering what is in my weapons. It is true, you creatures, all of you, can't stand steel. It makes you weak."

He held a strand of her hair, twirling it around his fingers, as if taunting his new toy. He glided his knife down the lines of her back, tracing the roundness of her bottom to her long legs. He brought the knife back to her chest where he appreciated the soft roundness of her bosoms. Ulf got closer to her ears, biting the lobe to whisper his disgusting act.

"It's the blood of your sisters, twelve of them to be exact. Bathed in the full moon while it's red. I admit, not an easy process, but it was worth it. Easier to kill you bloody lot."

In a sudden twist, Revna opened her eyes, the sound of her sisters' cries waking her up. She was the only one left and she'd been sending demons to search for their killer. Now, he was here, and there was no way she would lose her life to him, too. She turned her right arm, lifting it up in the air, striking Ulf's neck.

His eyes opened wide before realizing long sharp talons had cut through his throat to his neck. Human blood trickled down Revna's face. She stood up while Ulf was still in her hands. A new resolve within her gave her enough strength to finish the fight.

"I should have known a murderer was in my woods."

She grabbed his neck and ripped his head off, blood showering her face and creating a pool around her feet.

Silence.

In pain, and unable to stand any longer, Reva fell to the ground in a daze. The pearl was protected, the woods were protected and the creatures who were light and dark were safe.

Revna looked to the moon and smiled. She had avenged the deaths of her sisters. She may have been the only one left, but she no longer felt alone.

THE TORRENT

BY

KALIVICTORIA

E very plant has its roots.

With branches that sink deep into the soil, with arms that are buried beneath the dirt—the plant grows above the surface to embrace its season, preparing itself for its future on the earth.

Twelve-year old Holly believes she is no different.

The young girl was named after a plant, after all; a tree, in fact. She has grown above the surface, as other humans do, but she has covered her boots in mud. Those red rubber boots have always embraced the mud.

This evening, Holly awakes to the sound of thunder. She sits up in her bed, holds her purple blanket to her heart, and her blue gaze dances beyond the view beside her pillow. Rain patters against the window, thumping against the glass to the sound of Holly's heartbeat. She turns away from the plummeting taps, smiles at another roll of thunder, and looks to her bedroom door, to the red rubber boots that sit beside the door frame.

Holly brings her feet to the bedroom floor, her feet covered in socks, her body draped in pajamas, but the young girl has planned this moment. She steps across the cold wooden floor to the dresser, her hand excitedly grabbing the rain coat that's still damp from yesterday's adventure. She steps to her red rubber boots, and feels secure within the mud-covered shoes.

She holds her breath as she opens her bedroom door, and she's careful to open it with ease, to stifle the sound of the creaks from the wood beneath her feet.

Her parents had warned her of the storm, just as they had warned her yesterday that she mustn't meet her friend River. River is reckless. But Holly trusts River. She enjoys the way

River is constantly moving, encouraging her imagination as they run through the forest and past the trees within it.

Holly's eyes are wide as she steps past her parents' bedroom door, and she balances her arms so her coat doesn't crinkle in the silence. She watches her steps along the floor, her boots tracing the wood with her footsteps, with mud, and she giggles silently at the sight of it. Her parents will yell at her for it, the young girl will smile at their voices, and the rules will never change as she grows.

For now, Holly makes her way into the kitchen, to the open plan of her home that peeks across wooden countertops, chairs, and side tables. The wooden roof above panels into the living room, to the dining room, to the bathroom. Holly only needs the back door.

The young girl inhales the smell of pine within her house before stepping past the fridge. The white appliance hums into her ear, competing with the sound of plummeting rain beside it. The weather beating against the back door makes Holly's heart beat faster.

She reaches for the metal knob, her pale knuckles thinning from the cold against her palm as she holds the door for a moment.

Just one moment.

Then, she pulls.

Thunder crashes into the sky above, lightning casts a vibrant glow into the ground below, and Holly steps into the pattering rain across her maple patio. The back door snaps shut and thunder strikes again, and Holly's breath whisks into the air as she walks across the maple wood toward maple stairs.

To mud.

Five wooden steps keep her from the mushy ground, technically four because one of the steps is broken. Holly had jumped onto it one day and broken it.

She decides to jump across it again.

She smiles at the squelch beneath her boots, at the rain hitting her coat, and she looks ahead toward the brush of leaves and branches that await her. She smiles because she's one step closer to River.

Reaching her friend requires a simple path. Holly needs to walk straight, to keep her head high, and to see the familiar markers that she and her friends have created within the woods.

The first marker can be reached within five minutes, past a rough patch of berry bushes and flower beds.

Holly focuses as she moves her boots across the muddy ground, clasping her hands together to keep her fingers warm. She keeps her hands close so she doesn't touch the poison ivy.

The plants here are rejoicing in the water across their branches. Holly can smell it. The air is damp, thick as it enters her nostrils, and the tree leaves are strong, helping the wind sing its whipping tune across the forest floor. The chilling song is sung across Holly's skin, but if she keeps moving, she'll warm eventually. Father had taught her that.

The red rubber boots squelch again. This time, against softer ground. Fertilized ground. Holly turns her body to the right, holding up her head and a hand to her eyes so she can see the berry bushes, the flower beds.

Blueberries or blackberries—it's hard to tell from the rain. But Holly has walked this path a number of times, and she looks to the flower bed to find the first marker of her path.

Instead, she finds her friend, Rose.

"Holly you must turn around!" Rose exclaims, but Holly steps closer to her friend.

Holly ignores how her smaller and more delicate friend shivers within the wind, bending down to hold her friend's hand.

"Holly, you must go home!" Rose warns. "The storm is too treacherous today, even more treacherous than yesterday. We cannot play!"

"I think we can!" Holly simply laughs, a smile on her face. "I thought *you thought* water was refreshing."

"But when it beats like this, it is frightening. And I am so cold. Aren't you cold?" asks Rose, and Holly shakes her head.

"Why are you out in this storm? You should go home!"

"I have to meet River. Won't you come along, Rose?" Holly asks, and Rose shakes her head, the action equating to a shiver beneath the rain.

"I must stay here, Holly. You know that," Rose says.

As the girl with red rubber boots places her hand onto a tree, the bark torn and wet beneath her fingers, Holly turns back to Rose, her fingers gripping the marker at the sound of Rose's voice.

"Are you sure you don't want to go home?" Rose calls out. "Won't your parents want you home?"

Holly laughs at the question, and she calls back to her friend with a smile on her face. "Goodbye, Rose!"

S*quish* goes Holly's boot as she takes a step forward, and *squish* goes the other boot as Holly takes another step. She continues her journey into the wet forest, the air turning crisp within her mouth, her body starting to produce heat.

Thunder crashes above and Holly finds herself blinking profusely at the sight before her, blinking away the water from her eyes. She pauses her journey for a moment, bringing a hand to her face to wipe away her blurry gaze. She looks ahead to find her friend, Conifer.

"Holly?" the gruffy figure asks. "Holly, is that you?"

"Hello, Conifer!" Holly greets, her lips instantly turning into a smile as she trudges across the forest floor.

Conifer's eyes widen at the sight of Holly, taking in her raincoat and her muddy boots.

"My, my, Holly! You're getting all wet, and all dirty! You should go home!" Conifer exclaims.

Holly shakes her head.

"You sound like Rose," Holly says, "But I must meet River. River is waiting for me."

"In this storm?" Conifer asks, and Holly nods. "I don't think even River is out in this storm today."

"River must be!" Holly says, her lips pursing at Conifer doubt. "Only River would understand how cool this storm is to me."

"But what of your parents?" asks Conifer. "Aren't you cold? Shouldn't you go home?"

"Goodbye, Conifer!" Holly sighs, stepping past another friend who expresses concern rather than excitement.

"Goodbye, Holly!" Conifer calls, but Holly doesn't turn around to see her friend say the words.

She continues her journey to River, and she doesn't place her hand on the second marker as she goes. She ignores the second tree with broken bark.

Thunder and lightning snap into the forest, and Holly flinches at the sound, her eyes nearly closed from the rain. She pauses again to wipe her face, and wipes it three or four times, pulling on her boots as they sink an inch into the ground.

The third marker should be close, and River should be just past it, waiting to run around with Holly like the pair had done yesterday.

Holly sucks in a breath between her chilled cheeks, her nose feeling stuffy, her breaths slowing into a wheeze. Walking this far into the forest has never been this hard, and as thunder cracks above the forest once again, Holly brushes the realization off.

None of it matters—the cold in the air, the heaviness of the forest air or the mud. Holly will throw away her problems as soon as she sits herself next to River.

Holly smiles as she thinks of River, and she wears that content smile when she finds the third marker. Her mighty friend Oak holds the marker in his hand.

"Holly, you look so cold!" Oak greets, hair flopping about in the wind, the strands whirling around his brown eyes as they hold Holly's mischievous gaze.

"Where are you off to today?" asks Oak.

"I'm going to see River," Holly replies. "I know it is cold, but River and I will keep warm. We always keep warm."

"But the storm rages tonight," Oak replies. "Mustn't you go home? Aren't your parents worried?"

"My parents don't know I'm here," Holly admits.

She nearly winces from the words, but her eyes flutter widely from a sudden idea.

"I'll have mother's soup when I get back! Would you like some as well?"

"Mother's soup? Why, of course!" Oak says, but Holly watches as the smile in his voice slips into a serious mutter. "You should return to Mother now. She has made soup for dinner tonight, yes?"

"And the night before," Holly says, and Oak chuckles.

"Return to your mother, Holly. Her soup will keep you warm."

"But what about you? What about River?" Holly asks.

"River isn't out tonight. The weather is too dangerous. Maybe River will be out tomorrow," says Oak, but Holly shrugs.

"I think he will be out tonight."

Holly steps past Oak. She doesn't touch the broken bark in his grasp.

"Goodbye, Holly!" Oak calls after her, but Holly doesn't turn around until she's ten trees away.

She never realized Oak's height until tonight.

Thunder cackles over head, the sound echoing into the ground below. Lightning flashes above, casting a vibrant glow into the sky. Holly's ears perk at the sound of the rain, the way it competes against the sound of flowing water.

Her red rubber boots pick up their pace across the mud, and she rushes toward her friend River and his joyous shouts of delight.

Instead, Holly finds someone else.

"Hello, Holly," the stranger says kindly.

Their breaths are fast, as if they've already been running for some time. And as the thunder cracks overhead and the branches glisten from the glare of lightning, the stranger seems to smile at remnants of the storm.

But Holly no longer wears a smile.

"Where's River?" Holly asks, and the stranger shrugs.

"I've never met River... Are they a friend of yours?"

"Yes," Holly says, and she takes a step back, an action that doesn't go unnoticed.

"We can still play," says the stranger.

"We can?" Holly furrows her brows.

"Sure," says the stranger. "We can do what you usually do with River. I'll try my best to act the same."

Holly pushes her weight onto one side of her leg, biting her cheek as she stares at the stranger.

"I am a friend," the stranger says, the sound of their voice drowning out beneath the wind, almost sad. "I don't have many friends."

The stranger sulks from the revelation, and Holly tilts her head. It's not like her to turn away from adventure. And though River is the person she normally plays with, River isn't the only person she can play with.

There are days when Holly plays with Rose, though the two remain closer to home. Her parents like Rose.

There are also days when Holly plays with Conifer, and her parents have always called Conifer a good friend. A sturdy friend, like Oak.

Holly's parents always feed Oak.

This evening, Holly chooses to smile at her new friend, and her new friend smiles back, letting out a shout of delight as Holly begins to race against it. This friend is faster than River, louder than River, and it doesn't wait for Holly as she begins to sink into the mud, slowing her steps.

"Wait!" Holly calls, but the stranger doesn't wait for Holly.

They don't turn to Holly as she slips onto the forest floor. They don't slow their pace as Holly's hands claw into the mushy dirt, attempting to clutch onto the nearest branch or twig or root so she can remain above the surface.

This friend isn't River, and this friend pulls Holly under.

Holly's cry clashes against the sound of thunder, and she feels buried within her raincoat, buried beneath rain drops, the flow of water and the cold. Even her boots feel cold.

Holly's arms flail around her, her legs and her breath failing her as well. She can't wipe the water away from her face fast enough, she can't fight the pull her new friend has on her body. She can't fight the way her friend pulls her lower and lower into the earth.

Holly cries beneath the waves, the smell of the forest air absent from her lungs. The feeling of freedom gone from her skin and beneath her feet. Her lungs burn, an unusual burn that she's never felt before, and her eyes go wide because she's never felt so restricted.

Holly closes her eyes so she doesn't have to feel it.

She's no longer connected to the ground, she's no longer attached to the forest floor. Instead, she's being carried away, roots and all, and her heart pounds to the sound of the waves. Her heart slows because this season will come to an end. She can't cry because the stranger who's dragged her from her roots laughs around her. That laugh drowns Holly's despair. That laugh tells Holly that the stranger thinks this is fun.

Holly should have listened to her friends.

She should have listened to Rose, the familiar flower that her mother had planted in the summertime. She should have listened to Conifer, the friend and lively bush that her father had known when he was a child. A bush that grows in the fall.

Holly should have listened to Oak.

Oak holds the third marker of the forest on his belly, his bark broken like his brothers closer to Holly's house. He provides shade for Holly during the springtime, and Holly's stomach clenches because she'll never get to eat soup with him during the winter.

Holly will never touch Oak's bark again.

Holly's cold now, too cold to move, too tired to try, and she thinks of River. Her breath stammers as she tries to talk to him, but he will never hear her.

This stranger has taken River's place, River's waves and pace. This stranger was never Holly's friend.

Holly releases a final breath, her ears perking as the stranger whispers against her skin.

"On your best days, I am a river. On your worst days, I am a stream. In the torrent, all plants wither. Under my waves, you will never leave."

Tale of

The Mystic Wood

By

Flor Ana

The sunlight still seemed to seep in through Lila's closed eyes. She laid face up on the warm grass, long blades tickling her skin, listening to the music that played through her headphones. It was Tuesday, her one-day-a-week trip to the park for adrenaline and grounding. It was her one-day-a-week escape from the noise of her brothers and sisters at home, the tediousness of school, and a chance to just connect with the nature that surrounded her in all its blue-green glory.

But The Mystic Wood wasn't your average park. In fact, anyone who had heard the stories would have thought Lila bold and a little crazy for venturing into its fields. The forest and its park and parts had been closed and left wild for over one hundred years now. But seventeen-year-old Lila didn't care. She didn't care for the horror stories of disappeared people, sinkholes, curses and anything else people decided to talk about when mentioning the wood. Something about it just always managed to captivate her, pulling her in. Perhaps it was the forest itself that called her name, drawing her into her own demise.

Mostly, Lila appreciated the fact that she got to be alone here, away from the drama, away from noise, with no one to bother her or ask anything of her.

Till today that was.

As Lila laid closed-eyed, for the first time in her handful of visits into The Mystic Wood, she felt a presence watching her. At first, she tried to shake it off, denying the possibility of anyone else being brave enough to jump the locked, barbed wire fence or crawl through the opening probably caused by a car ramming into it. Still, the feeling of being stared at was persisting and becoming unbearable. Suddenly, everyone's fears of what lay in the forest—murderers, bears, witches, alligators—began to fill her thoughts. What had begun as a peaceful lay in the grass, feeling the sun's heat on her fair skin quickly turned into a pounding heart and jumbled thoughts.

What the hell, she thought, rapidly sitting up from the grass, looking around.

And there he was.

A tall, tanned, lanky boy standing ten paces to her left.

She cursed at herself in her head for coming out here in the first place, fearing the boy might be some kind of manic killer.

But Lila kept her composure.

"Who are you and what are you doing here?" she said curiously, taking off her headphones and throwing them gently next to her bag.

She tried to hide how loud her heart was beating, how fast her breaths had become, and though the boy stood at a far enough distance to not be able to hear her slight panic, his staring and stillness only made her stomach quelch as her uneasiness increased.

Silence.

The boy shifted his weight from one leg to the other.

"I'm waiting," Lila spoke, standing up and wiping the dried grass off her ripped jeans before crossing her arms.

The boy finally talked.

"My... m-my name is... My name is Jax. I didn't know anyone came out here. I thought I'd be alone... I... I thought you were a ghost."

He chuckled at his own response as if he'd heard how absurd he sounded, but with Lila's pale skin and blue eyes, the only thing keeping her from truly looking like an apparition was a heartbeat and her fiery crimson hair.

"Sorry to disappoint, but I'm very much alive," she said, holding her hands up as if guilty.

He snickered, slipping his hands into the pockets of his corduroy green pants.

"I didn't mean to interrupt, you know," Jax said, gesturing at the grass and Lila's discarded bag while getting closer. "You just caught me by surprise."

"Yeah, well, same," she said, a mixture of fear and annoyance in her tone.

He smiled at her, expecting her to smile back, but when her scrunched face remained unchanged, his smile quickly faded away.

Ah, I shouldn't have bothered this girl. Jeez, she looks upset.

In her many times venturing into The Mystic Wood, the only souls she had encountered belong to raccoons, stray cats and the occasional chipmunk. In fact, the woods themselves were riddled with intricate, untouched spiderwebs that remained intact, unbothered. The fact that this appeared to no longer be a place to just be left alone left a bad taste in her mouth.

To anyone who knew her, Lila appeared sweet… until she opened her mouth or made any kind of face that wasn't resting. Still, Jax didn't seem to be intimidated by her, though that was what she wanted. She wore a Rage Against The Machine T-shirt, ripped black jeans and platformed Converse, all the looks of an angsty teen.

And yet something about her, in a way, drew him in. Maybe it was the fact that she was much shorter than him, smelled of strawberries or had such fair skin that he could see her blue-green veins with ease.

Maybe she is a ghost, Jax thought, looking at her with curiosity as she remained looking at him with distaste.

"You still haven't answered my question. What are you doing here?" she said with arms still crossed, a twang of annoyance with every spoken syllable.

He decided to play her at her own game.

"I could ask you the same thing. You do know this place is closed, right? Off limits?" he said with a bit of authority, folding his arms as if to mimic her stance.

"Well, you're here, too, aren't you? So, that makes us both in for trouble if we get caught in here."

"Actually," Jax said, pulling out a badge and clearing his throat. "I'm a park ranger, so..."

Lila laughed, smiling for the first time since their encounter.

"Wait, how old are you?"

While Jax was tall, he had a baby face if Lila had ever seen one.

"Nineteen," he responded, aware of what she was thinking.

Lila could hear the twang in his voice, like if suddenly he was of high importance. Despite the fact he was older, had a badge and a supposed title, she was not easily impressed.

"And how old are you? And what's your name?" Jax asked when Lila stayed quiet, seeming to analyze him.

"Lila," she answered. "And age doesn't matter," she responded, biting her cheek.

Then, she smirked.

"So, uh... your boss knows you're here?" she questioned him, thinking she already knew the answer—and she did.

Jax's eyes widened, the brown in them on the verge of oozing out.

"Well... no... he doesn't."

Lila shrugged her shoulders, staying quiet, thinking there would be more to his response. When he didn't say anything, she turned to her stuff and picked up her headphones, bag and book that had fallen out from the open zipper. *Alice in Wonderland*. A pink leatherback edition. She stuffed it quickly back in her beat up pouch, hoping Jax hadn't had a chance to see what book it was.

She began to walk back towards the section of the fence she had jumped when the subtle crack in Jax's voice caused her to stop.

"Wait!" he said. "You don't have to leave."

There was almost a plea to his voice. Perhaps, he was just as drawn to the mystic as she was. Lila thought for a moment, her back turned to him.

"Why are you here?" she asked once more, this time with demand and better authority than he had when he pulled out his park ranger badge.

She'd won the game she didn't even know they were playing.

"Okay, okay. Easy there... I'm here because... I'm here because I was planning on going in."

Jax pointed into the woods, the entrance a web of overgrown shrubs and gnats.

Lila looked into the beaten path that lay still with tangled trees. She scuffed in this disbelief.

"Have you ever gone in?" he asked, pulling her eyes away from the forest and onto his.

Lila shook her head, looking at Jax with eyes that said, *Come on, look at that place.*

She had been driving to The Mystic Wood, parking her car two blocks down near a rundown laundromat, and just sitting in the outskirts of the forest, in the park and overgrown grass, since she'd discovered its location three months earlier after another supposed trespasser had gone missing. In the three months that had passed, the young man lost to the woods had yet to be found, but Lila didn't fear the woods and its shrubbery. She'd just always figured the people who supposedly got lost did so because they went too far in. The Mystic Wood covered forty-five acres of land. Forty-five acres that Lila presumed were filled with maze-like abandoned paths, creeping crawlers, and who knows what else.

While she enjoyed the eeriness and adrenaline that came with being somewhere she knew she shouldn't be, going into the actual forest always left her feeling nauseous.

As tough-as-nails as Lila wanted to seem and be, the truth was she was terrified of stepping into The Mystic Wood and never finding her way out. Still, she was extremely curious as to why Jax wanted in.

"Have you ever gone in before?" she asked, trying to seem uninterested.

"Just once… and I made it out, didn't I?" Jax said jokingly, attempting to lighten the tension at the thought of what the woods would hold.

Lila dropped her shoulders, finally admitting to herself that Jax was not some young serial killer and that he was probably harmless.

"Yeah," she grinned. "Looks like you did make it out alright."

Jax smiled at her, feeling like he'd slightly won over a bit of Lila's trust.

As ease and breeze filled the air, their moment of comfort with one another quickly turned.

Fog began to roll through the forest, filling the ground until the grass was barely visible. Gray clouds filled the sky as if a storm were brewing.

Lila and Jax looked at each other, thoughts cluttering their minds though either refused to speak.

Then, Jax broke the silence.

"Uh… I don't think it was supposed to rain today…"

But the tough girl facade was over.

"That's it. I'm out."

Lila slung her bag over her arm and fiddled for her keys. As they jingled, she heard the voice of someone else behind her. A woman.

"You're not going anywhere."

Her voice was sharp, a demeanor that could raise the dead if she simply tried.

Lila stopped in her tracks, silenting putting the keys back in her bag. She looked over to Jax who now seemed he was really seeing a ghost as all the blood drained from his honey-colored face. She turned slowly, heart pounding in her ears louder than when she had met Jax and palms sweating under closed fists. As she faced the woman, Lila, intrigued and anxious, just stared.

She was magnificent. A tall woman with a fly amanita crown that seemed as if it were protruding from her skull while other blush-pink-colored mushrooms grew from her shoulder blades. Her eyes were a fluorescent emerald-citrine, capable of piercing souls, and her hair, a wavy, thick chocolate brown, reached below her breasts. Her skin was iridescent and sun-spotted, sparkling like diamonds in the sun. Still, you could see blue-green veins coming through her flesh.

"What is your name?" she said elegantly, as a queen addressing her court.

Her question was directed to Lila who stood before her.

Lila gulped, ignoring the chills running through her.

"Lila," she said, hiding as best she could the tremor in her voice.

"No," the woman replied, unaccepting of her answer. "What is your real name?"

Lila's sky blue eyes opened wide.

How could she know? No. I refuse to give into this.

She stayed quiet, staring. But she felt a pull at her throat as she and the woman locked eyes, the emerald-citrine light in them forcing the words, her name, to escape her. She tried to swallow it down, pressing her tongue to the roof of her mouth.

Finally, she gave in as she began to taste copper.

"Lilac!" she screamed in agony.

Even Jax's face was riddled with fear. Lila caught her breath.

"My name is Lilac, but I prefer Lila… if you please."

She curtsied, feeling foolish, but hoping this act of somewhat respect would make the woman go easier on her.

What is this woman? Lila thought. *Is she a witch?*

Then, as if reading her thoughts, the woman spoke up. "I am a witch, dear, and I know far more than you do about the magic that runs through me."

The witch took a deep breath and turned to Jax.

"And you, what is your name?"

The words came out like vomit.

"Jax… Ja… Jackson. Jackson is my name," he blurted, his final words almost faint.

Lila scuffed, as if she wasn't afraid herself.

Wimp, she thought, still trying to hold on to her toughness.

"And what is your name?" she questioned the woman, a slight bit of sass in her tone.

The witch cackled.

"I have many names, child."

"Well, there must be one you prefer…"

"I guess there is. Call me Armillaria."

Isn't that the scientific name of a honey mushroom? Jax questioned, the park ranger in him escaping his thoughts.

"It is, Jackson. You're smart. I like you. I like you both. You're… different."

Lila and Jax looked at each other, worry in their eyes that they were about to be eaten or enslaved.

"Your company is pleasant. Come with me, children," Armillaria said, turning around, her dress twirling as she did, and heading for the misty woods.

"I'm not going in there," Lila blurted, a tinge of disgust in her voice.

The witch moved close to her, rapidly, almost floating in the air, and looked deeply into her eyes. The emerald-citrine were spirals, pools of crystal to get lost in.

"I did not ask you, Lilac," she said, almost a whisper, grabbing Lila's chin.

Jax stood still, witnessing the scene before him.

What is she doing? he thought. *Is she trying to get herself killed? Get us killed? Ah, that's right you can hear me. I'm sorry.*

Lila remained silent. Her pale color had left her, turning her a slight shade of blue.

The three walked quietly into the woods, the witch untouched by the intertwined roots that poked out of the ground or by the thick silk webs of red and black jagged spiders. Where Armillaria walked with grace, Lila and Jax walked with caution, avoiding depressions, puddles of plumage and spiked trunks that could stab like a knife.

Even their thoughts had fallen silent, nervous to think anything the witch might hear.

Lila was the first to speak up, ducking a wide branch that disrupted the path.

"So, Armillaria… What's your story? Witch of the forest or wicked witch of the east?"

Her voice was casual, like if she hadn't been threatened by the woman fifteen minutes before. Jax just continued walking silently, bending over tangled vines that would have caught his neck. He was bewildered at both ladies, Lila for her bravery and Armillaria for everything else.

Armillaria sighed, a hint of melancholy on her breath.

"Very funny, Lilac" she replied unamused. "I am the witch. I guess of this forest, but heavens, not by choice. I'm cursed to roam these grounds. Have been doing so for over a thousand years."

Woah, thought Jax. *That's a long time.*

"It has been a long time, Jackson. Too long if you ask me."

Lila wanted to keep probing her, but didn't know what words to use, what to say at all. And in that moment, she'd forgotten all about Armillaria's ability to read minds.

"Let's stop here, children," the witch said, pausing abruptly.

She looked around as if she could see more than met the human eye. Then, she pressed her hand to the earth they stood on, closing her eyes for only a second.

With her exhale, three toadstools rose from the ground, large enough to sit on. One elevated a silver feather that then sunk to the ground.

Jax and Lila stood amazed at what they'd just witnessed—real magic. They took a seat, unsure if to be in awe or terrified.

"Let me tell you a story," she began, crossing one leg over the other and looking off into the distance, figuring out where to start.

"Many, many moons ago, I was like you. Human. Full of life and always with a curiosity for nature that would draw me out of bed and into the forest every day. I used to love foraging, picking mushrooms to eat and to create paint with. Then, one day, I seemed to have picked up the wrong mushroom."

Armillaria paused, wanting to see the reactions on Jax and Lila's faces.

"Well, what happened?" Jax pushed her to continue.

"It was a pink mushroom—blush pink, to be exact. And I'd never seen anything like it before. It smelled of cinnamon, so strong that you could smell it from... well, quite a distance. So, I decided to pick it..."

She looked as if she was filled with regret, anger bottled up at her past self.

"So, you picked a mushroom and mother earth cursed you?" Lila said, only half jokingly.

"It wasn't that simple, child. I *ate* the mushroom, and its properties began to mesh with my own. Our cells became one. It was a merger I had never asked for!"

Her crescendoing voice brought fear into Jax's eyes, concerned with what she was capable of doing.

Lila cleared her throat, darting her eyes to the dirt that clung to her shoes.

"What happened next?" she asked, wanting to know more.

"I... I tried everything to get it out, the mycellium's thoughts sometimes louder than my own. But I couldn't. There was nothing that could be done... So, I stayed in the forest, trying to find a cure or something. But I guess it was too late. I can't escape the woods. Now, I'm just cursed to roam, stuck here as the mycelium networks that run underground keep me here, like an autonomous plant still needing to be with her roots."

They remained silent as they noticed the light in Armillaria's eyes slightly dull. Jax rubbed his hands together, noticing the time on his watch. 3:33.

Is time froz— he stopped his thoughts, his eyes darting to the witch, fearing she'd heard him.

But Armillaria was stuck in her own head, her poise now hanging on by only a thread. Then, annoyance struck her face like a slap.

"And I try to be kind to you bloody lot!" she hollered to no one in particular.

This caught Lila's attention. She raised her eyebrows.

"Wait, what do you mean by that?"

"You children, always sneaking in. Gawking like birds, disrupting the little peace I have, picking at the mind-altering mushrooms that do not belong to you."

There was fire in her eyes, annoyance and animosity.

Lila was bewildered, her heart pacing three times faster than it just had before. She tried controlling her thoughts, making sure Armillaria couldn't pinpoint where her mind was.

Armillaria was calming down, her wave of rage subsiding back into the ocean. She sighed.

"But I like *you*, children. You pass through the closed gate, but always stop where the trees begin. I've been watching you both. Silenting listening to music or reading," she looked at Lila, "or drawing," she looked at Jax, "neither of your presences have ever managed to disturb me."

Armillaria smiled, happy that her new pets hadn't had the courage to walk into her home uninvited.

Lila couldn't take it anymore, her leg twitching as she held her hands in prayer to her mouth.

"All those missing people… the hikers, the kids… Do you know anything about that?"

Things were finally clicking for Jax, his own leg beginning to tick and twitch. He just *oooooo'd* in his mind, trying to not think at all. Armillaria rolled her eyes.

"Hm, yes… those squealers and gawkers… getting all loud in my neck of town… I did them a favor, really…"

Lila's eyes wanted to water, fearing her own death was approaching, but she did her best to remain strong and keep her faith.

"You killed them?" she asked, her voice almost a whisper as one solid tear escaped her eye socket.

"Oh, heavens, Lilac! I didn't kill anyone! I'm not a murderess."

Lila didn't know if she believed her. Just three months earlier, another person had gone missing. What were before just conspiracy theories and misguided connections to the ominous woods at the edge of town now actually had meat to their bones, and she was standing in front of the person, the *thing*, responsible for the pain of so many others.

"If you didn't kill them, what did you do with them?" Lila voiced, her throat scratchy with every vowel.

"Have you not been paying attention, dear? Do you not have a vivid imagination? I said they gawked like birds… So, I did what I had to do and turned them into birds."

Armillaria smiled, satisfied with her actions, triumphant.

Jax and Lila glanced at each other from the corners of their eyes, both hearts beating loudly in their chests, on the verge of coming out through their ears. What to do remained unknown in their empty thoughts. Then, Lila had an idea.

*I wonder if she feeds them? What time is it? I have
school tomorrow. I smell like sweat. What kind of birds?
Does she wish she could be a bird? I wish I could fly. I'm
hungry. I'm thirsty. Is she planning on turning us into bir—*

"Enough, Lilac!" Armillaria shouted, covering her ears
with her veiny, bony fingers.

"I have no plans for it, but if you persist with these
pesky thoughts, I might just change my mind."

"Sorry… Just a lot… in my head," Lila responded, her
voice seemingly small, a hint of tiredness.

Jax raised his eyebrows, looking at them both in
confusion. His stomach growled, louder than he had
probably expected it to. Lila giggled at the monstrous sounds
that escaped him.

"Ah, I've had enough of you two for one day. Be gone."
"Wait!"

Armillaria raised her arms as if about to do an
incantation, but Lila's shout made her lower her arms slowly
as they once again locked eyes.

"Yes, child? What now? What do you want?" Armillaria
said, anger and aggravation lingering after she spoke.

Lila cleared her throat, putting her hair behind her ears
as if to show Armillaria all of the details of her face, all of
the honesty that was just about to pour out. With her heart
beating fast, and knowing she wouldn't be returning to The
Mystic Wood, she knew she had to do something, say
something,

"Look, I'm not a thousand years old, or cursed to stay in
an abandoned forest, or anything that you've experienced…
but I do know what it's like to be young and the adrenaline
and fun that comes with being somewhere you're not
supposed to be."

Armillaria took a deep breath whilst closing her eyes.

"What is the point of what you're saying, Lila?"

Lila raised her head a little, lifted her eyebrows. She'd called her Lila. She was actually listening to her. Her heart patted lightly.

"The point I'm making is that…"

Lila stopped, her blue eyes slightly bulging as she looked for the right words to say while containing her thoughts. She took a deep breath.

"The point I'm making is that you were young once. I know there's anger in your heart, but those people who just wandered into the woods… they didn't know. They didn't know what you'd been through. They weren't thinking of your perspective, and… you weren't thinking of theirs."

Lila got up from the toadstool, signalling she was done. As soon as she rose, the makeshift mushroom chair quickly sank back down into the earth, leaving no trace, taking with it a small dirty, dusty blue feather. She slid her hands into the back pockets of her dirt-stained jeans.

Jax got up, too, eagerly making sure to look closely as the toadstool returned to the earth.

That was so cool! Ah, sorry, he thought, looking at Armillaria as he gritted his teeth.

She sighed.

"I suppose you're right. Thank you for sharing that."

Lila couldn't tell if she'd made some type of change in the witch, but there wasn't time to ponder. Armillaria raised her arms again, this time nothing stopping her from what she was about to do.

"Be gone!" she shouted, fluttering her fingers in the air like magic was coming out of each phalange.

Before Lila and Jax had time to panic about what the witch was going to do to them, the dried leaves around them swirled, encasing them in a vortex. Jax closed his eyes once all he saw were spinning leaves around him. Lila clenched her fists, unsure of if to try and punch her way out or just let go and let happen.

When the leaves subsided, falling back to the ground, they were at the outskirts of the forest. The same place they'd met hours earlier, Armillaria nowhere to be seen.

Lila exhaled air through her mouth with force, shifting her weight from one leg to the next before falling to the grass.

Realizing they were no longer in the cold, leafy vortex, Jax opened his eyes, seeing Lila in a sort of cat-cow position, digging her nails into the dirt. He looked around, searching for Armillaria thoroughly. When he finally gave in to the idea that she was really gone, he walked over to Lila and bent down next to her.

"Hey, you okay?"

She looked up at him, dirt on her cheeks and sweat gleaming.

"Yeah," she said, getting up. "I'm great."

She once again slung her bag across her body, holding on the strap at her side.

"You?"

"Well, I'm alive," Jax said smiling, his heart still pounding in his chest.

"Let me ask you something," Lila said.

"Yeah?" Jax responded, nerves tingling down his spine.

"You'd never gone in there before had you?"

Jax looked down, knowing he was being called out for having lied before, regretting his actions.

"No... and I'm sorry for not being honest about that... Just wanted to... impress you... I guess..."

Lila smoothly crossed her arms, a slight smile on her face.

"Oh you didn't think your badge had been that impressive in the first place?" she joked, and he laughed about it, too.

Suddenly, birds of all colors and sizes took to the skies, each producing their own call, all headed in different directions.

It was a beautiful sight, their colors so vivid against a setting sun.

Lila smiled, releasing the air she'd held in her chest.

She let them go… I hope they all find their way home.

She looked at Jax, a pout where she smiled.

"Don't you get it? She let them all go!"

"How can you be so sure?" he asked, worried that she might just release them to the skies before summoning them back.

"I have faith," Lila responded. "I have faith that she did the right thing."

They walked to the fence, climbing one by one carefully over the barbed wire, birds still taking to the skies above them.

Once on the other side of The Mystic Wood, they went to part ways, beginning to walk in different directions, but Jax stopped for a moment, turning back with a jog.

"Hey, Lila!"

She turned around casually, her hands back on the strap of her bag across her chest.

"Um… It was nice meeting you."

"Oh, yeah, you too."

"I hope to see you again?"

"Yeah… we'll see… just not here…"

He breathed out through his nose playfully.

"Yeah, that sounds good."

She brushed her hand against his shoulder.

"You take care, ranger boy. Don't get yourself into any trouble in these neck of woods."

Lila spoke in her best boy scout voice. They laughed.

"So, really, how old are you? You were pretty brave back there."

"I'm seventeen, and yeah, definitely braver than you," she said, biting her lip.

"Well, stay brave," Jax said, looking into her eyes.

No one spoke anything else. What needed to be said had been said. What needed to happen had happened.

Jax waved to her as he turned around and began his walk to his car. Lila, on the other hand, stood in place for a moment, looking through the fence for any sight of Armillaria.

While she couldn't see her, something told Lila she was present. She looked up, watching over as the skies cleared again, only a bird or two still flying slowly, only a few drops of sunlight remaining. Lila held on to the fence, bowing her head.

"Thank you," Lila whispered. "Thank you for seeing things through a different perspective, through someone else's eyes."

A Modern Metamorphosis

By

Kim Rashidi

The mist of pine and the crickets of night creatures precede the forest hidden deep behind the city's lights. They shine with false pretenses, begging pedestrians to come in and have their world altered for a night. Behind neon signs for virtual reality bars, a green ambiance full of mystery calls her name. She's walking behind a man in a trench coat. He's not too tall, but looms high enough to be as ominous as the scene seems. He stops at a bodega, his voice monotone, and asks for a pack of cigarettes. She pulls up her collar and walks past him as the tender's slow movements stall him. She feels herself drawn by the limbs like a marionette puppet whose actions are out of its control. Though she doesn't know exactly where she's gravitating towards, she's known this pull before, deep in childhood, just young enough to remember touching a trunk, falling to her feet. Darkness. Then, better. It was all better after that. So, it's no surprise that she leans all in, guided by her intuition.

Gliding through the city, she makes eye contact with no one. It's not easy where she lives, the overcrowding and the money-hungry people trying to sell things at every corner are difficult enough to avoid. Mix in the narrow streets plus the out-of-order city rides, and vices are a hellscape she can't escape.

Gliding through her life, she makes efforts not to be lonesome. She hosts an array of dinner parties, gathers acquaintances, drinks the night away, and acts like she doesn't pretend. She fakes it, almost always—liking the people around her. She doesn't know yet that she's afraid they'll leave, so she stops herself from loving them too much. She meets people at book clubs and at mandatory work trainings where they learn how to treat people fairly, but they never seem to stick. She blames who people usually blame: her parents.

She can smell it stronger: the pine. As if the scent were her leash, she follows closely and, soon enough, she arrives. The urge to be there is overwhelming now, and she doesn't know why she's been summoned, but she doesn't see any groves nearby. She thinks an entrance is somewhere, if only she can find it behind the artificial plants housing abandoned bird feeders. The trench coat man isn't far behind. She needs to enter, and she needs to enter now. They exchange a quick glance, his face stern, she knows she'll have to greet him in a moment, and butterflies swarm inside her stomach. Just then, the earth beneath sucks her in. She falls with relief on her shoulders, nearly floating to the earth's core.

A patchy green space opens up, bouncy as ever, and receives her warmly. On her back, she looks above to the tree branches and leaves and fruits and bushes shrouding the view of what's beyond. As if by routine, she gets up, sheds her coat, dusts her jeans, and looks for something she doesn't quite remember.

She walks towards a tree and touches its bark, but nothing comes of it. It's soft to the touch, almost smooth and smells of the flames of fire. She continues, in search of something else. Modestly sized cottage-esque homes with stones for walls and castle towers meant for battle decorate empty lots. An old woman tends to her garden, humming the tune of an old song.

"Be a dear and fill up my watering can by the stream, love," the old lady says, certain of the outcome.

She does not take a moment to consider. She knows she must oblige. Drawing close to the woman, her stomach clenches at the look of the woman's face. There is nothing wrong with it, not even a wrinkle out of place. She reaches for the watering can, determined to exchange a touch while in the process, just to confirm reality. The old lady feels warm, sweaty even, and just as she grabs the watering can, the lady smiles.

"My youth depends on it," the woman says, sounding more like a reminder than anything else.

The forest looks different since her last visit, cheerier in a way. Though she'd seen people before, none of them had spoken to her then. It's day in the forest, and she wonders how.

There is no sun, surely we are underground, she thinks to herself, *perhaps the earth's core has its own light, refracting what's above, perhaps it's always day here, despite what stories of the underworld may say.*

Looking above, trying to figure out how it's so bright, she trips over a tree root snaking across the forest floor. Her palms and feet pace each other faster than learned in babyhood. Once she has put enough distance between herself and the awakened roots, she observes. The root moves slowly toward another, and when they reach each other, they intertwine as if to hold hands. Now eloped, they remain in stillness, as trees typically do.

At the stream, she catches her reflection, herself as a young adult. Her hair is long and brown, before the damage of years of bleaching, her nose buttoned as always, full lips, and large eyes.

Not much has changed, she thinks.

The last time she entered this hypnotizing forest, her mother had dropped her off at a friend's house and hadn't even waited for her to get inside before driving off. She'd rung the doorbell, but had been sucked into the earth before the door opened. She remembers that, last time, her reflection hadn't mirrored back to her in the water.

She fills the watering can, carefully steps over the united roots, and walks back towards the old lady's cottage. The lady grabs the vessel from her and spills a few drops on herself before pouring the rest on her flowers. The old lady turns back to thank her, and her wrinkles have visibly shrunk, yet the flowers immediately bloom in front of her eyes.

"I remember you from before," she says.

"Why did you come?" the now middle-aged woman asks.

"It wasn't exactly on purpose… then or now.

"Oh. You poor thing! How old were you before?"

"Eight."

"My dear, you were far too young for any of us to guide you. We could barely see you then," the woman says with complete sincerity.

"I have to go," she responds, walking off towards the tree that she now remembers is waiting for her.

What did the woman mean they could barely see me, she wonders.

She notices she's pressing her nails too far into her palms trying to figure this out and rolls her shoulders back, trying to ease the tension of the unknown. She knows the forest takes you back to a time you need to understand the most. And last time, at eight, she'd witnessed her birth.

Perhaps they hadn't seen me because I had yet to exist, she thinks to herself.

An old man in the distance catches her eye, he shakes his head no, as if to respond to the possibility she just thought of. He turns away and climbs a tree with more strength than one would imagine he has.

She tries to summon the memory of direction, which is most definitely not her strong suit. She turns towards a tree whose bark looks particularly like fingerprints. Her hands are now at the tree, feeling for grooves that fit her palms. As if guided by muscle memory, she presses into the crevice of a branch, and the trunk releases a sap. She looks around to ensure her safety and sees the man watching her from atop a tree in the distance. A bird flies towards him and joins him in his new homestead. He nods at her to reassure her safety, so she tips her head sideways and opens her mouth, welcoming the sweet nectar of the tree.

It flows down her throat with no resistance and she imagines it turning her soft insides into gold upon contact. She rests at the base of the tree, her back pressing into its prints and closes her eyes, as if to meditate before it all starts.

Again, she sees the time of her birth. This time, with less details filled in. She hears how her father could not bear to hear her cries and had seen her for the last time when it was only the first as well. She recalls how much she hated him, and the story her mother had spun about his abandonment, how she said he didn't care at all. She sees what she saw before, how he'd had to leave that day in the hospital because her cries reminded him of a daughter he'd lost. He'd blamed himself time and time again, going through life bitter with regret. She sees him at night in bed, talking to the daughters he never saw grow up, apologizing for his faults, and surrendering to the nightmares that call him to sleep.

She remembers after she'd witnessed all this that first time, she was okay, she'd felt stronger, less resentful. At eight, she'd learned that sometimes people have to leave behind the people they love.

A drowsiness kicks in and she scoops down lower on the tree trunk, her eyes bat in pleasure and she gives in to the calls. Deep in the unknown, the man climbs down and approaches her, offering his hand.

"You're safe here," he says, "I knew you'd come if I called your name enough times."

"Who are you?" she asks.

"You see me in my human form, though I seem generic and could be any man—"

She cuts him off, "*What* are you?"

"There is no word for what I am. I am the part of you that knows all that you can access at any time. I am the world and the cosmos crumbled into one," he answers, as if these words are easily palatable.

She examines his eyes, which reflect herself clearly, and checks the curve of his smile for a mistake that would falsify him. The strands of his hair look perfectly crafted, swooping in a swift motion to one direction. She reaches for him, once again ensuring reality just as she did with the old woman.

"We are all real," he says, anticipating her question. "We are guides to help you heal."

"Why didn't you speak to me last time? Where were you then?" she asks.

"You were young enough to let your imagination guide you then. I appeared to you in bird form, in songs, and in food. You trusted me as whatever I was, but now your age defies me. Had I been any of the forms I've been before, you'd write me off, call yourself crazy."

"Okay, so let's get on with it. What do I need to learn now?" she says, sounding almost annoyed.

He picks up on her stubborn nature and knows exactly what she needs.

"Ah. I cannot tell you so simply this time. Search within yourself to find what you lack. I will help you after that," he says, motioning to an impeccable backdrop of the scenes of her life, all strewn together and divided into chapters in between trees marking her life with plaques of ages and phases she's been through.

Now, more obviously annoyed, she turns away from the man and walks down a literal memory lane. She sees herself at nine falling behind in math, crying after every class, asking for help from her mom, and being bewildered by her response: *I'm busy.*

Her thirteen-year-old self is being offered a beer at a friend's house, she accepts and spends the night throwing up. At fifteen, her race is criticized, and she doesn't understand what's being made fun of, what they ridicule is normal to her.

She's seventeen and her body is over-sexualized. She tires of reading about who's hot and who's not, finding herself atop a list with names she doesn't even recognize.

She sees her eighteen-year-old self and knows she needs to talk some sense into her. She approaches her newly adult self, staring into a mirror. She's in the bathroom of her mother's home, trying to conjure up the words to say that she looks good. Her self-confidence has been low, she's been filling her voids with self-help books, boozy nights, and time alone. So much time alone. She places her hand on her younger self's shoulder and tells her the friends that leave her were never friends at all. Her younger self rolls her eyes, opens the cabinet to rid her of her older image, and sits on the bathroom floor.

"It doesn't matter if they don't like you!" she says, trying to calm her younger self down.

"And why should I believe you? What are you? Thirty and still alone?" the younger one bites back.

She looks for the man, feeling like she's been played. Her younger self is a nightmare to deal with and she won't cooperate. The man is not in sight and she grows angry by his deceit. She shuts her eyes and wills herself back to consciousness, she's going to find this man and find out what this and he *really* are.

Immediately thirsty after jolting back into the forest of peculiar dreams, her throat feels as if it's shutting in on itself. She runs down to the stream and takes in gulp after gulp, imagining her insides previously gilded by the sap turning back into pink muscle and flesh. She reaches her hands into the water to cup some up to her face and wash away whatever awkward dream that was. She notices a tattoo suddenly on her wrist, one she got removed at nineteen after having been betrayed once again. The tattoo is of half a butterfly, the other half belonging to a girl she met that night she was in the bathroom, mustering up the confidence to go out.

Of course, she thinks, *the age-rewinding body of water.*

She searches for the man, ready to confront him and his lies. She thinks she'll find him and ask what kind of place this is. She'll say she has no interest in *talking* to her old self and demand to be set free.

The man is no longer perched atop the tree. Staring at the trees, she tries to make out if he's hidden behind the leaves or branches that shroud the "sky." Squinting her eyes, she sees a figure flutter, and out of the blurry distance, a butterfly emerges, floats down to her, and rests on her tattooed hand.

"Hello," she greets the kind creature, who remains unwavering from her body.

A flashback takes her by surprise. She sees herself at the parlor shop, flipping through laminated sheets of flash tattoos with this new girl she just met. One of them had had the idea to get matching tattoos, bonding them forever after the unbelievable night they'd just experienced. She had pointed to a butterfly that looked different from the rest, less cheesy in a sense.

"I'll get half, you get the other," she had said to Nadia, the new girl.

Nadia had nodded her head and proclaimed that she would bravely go first, since she *had* saved her life anyway. She didn't know where the confidence had come from to jump in and grab Nadia by the arm. Maybe luck had stricken her as if she were a lottery ticket played enough times to finally win.

Snapping out of the vision, she witnesses the butterfly flap its wings, almost pointing towards a kiosk serving drinks. She approaches the bar and places the winged piece of life by a bowl of sticky sap. The butterfly consumes it with grace, drinking it up slowly and delicately, then returns to her hand. Her heart feels tight, like it's pumping heavy metal instead of blood. She knows who the butterfly is, who the man was—she never forgave herself after that big loss.

Yes, she'd saved Nadia's life that night when an on-going truck had sped by. Nadia had not predicted its speed as she was trying to cross the road to buy her some water. In a quick motion, led by none other than her intuition, she'd grabbed Nadia's arm, yanking her back, both falling with a thud. They'd laughed it off, and Nadia had told her that she was glad she decided to come out after all. Nadia had remembered her birthday the next week and stopped by with tokens of her love: chocolates she'd half eaten and shoes she'd seen in the window of a shop close to where she'd saved her life. She thanked Nadia endlessly, adoring the new girl with awe. She'd mentioned her birthday and that she admired the shoes in passing, not expecting anyone to remember at all.

But it was as if fate had wanted Nadia dead or not in her life. Life would try to take her new best friend away from her whenever she wasn't looking. Car crashes, dangerous dives, and life-threatening encounters with strangers at bars had left Nadia stronger than she thought she was. Nadia's resilience is why, one day after a call, she'd expected everything to be alright. She'd minded her own business and taken too long. She'd stopped by a bodega, getting Nadia a drink she loved, and in the precious few minutes she'd spent hoping to cheer her up, she'd lost Nadia without getting to say goodbye.

She now sees that moment flash by. She witnesses Nadia in the park, chasing after a simple butterfly with music in her ears, unable to hear people warning her of an oncoming truck, as if the one that night they met wasn't enough. She grimaces at the scene, at the force of impact, at Nadia's skull hitting the ground, there's no blood yet and she's got some hope that Nadia will live, but she doesn't know why… Nadia has been dead for years.

Stepping out of the horrible vision, the butterfly now flies close to her face, landing on her nose. It flutters its wings as if to offer a kiss and flies off.

Still unresolved, she feels hurt that she's had to see that crime scene. Hearing about it all those years ago had been enough. Angry that she just relived that day, she pushes the bowl housing the sap away and its container shatters on the ground. She kneels to pick up the pieces, feeling regretful to have caused further harm, and she dips her finger into some sap, tasting what the butterfly had drunk up. With an overwhelming urge to sit down, she does so and hears a sound with no noise, a calling that has no form.

As if with images, static, thoughts, and smells, she senses these few words, "A goodbye wouldn't have even been enough. I'm glad we had our time."

Her eyes are filled with tears, and again, her regret looms in, scratching at her insides, finding a way to make her feel guilty. She shouldn't have gotten the tattoo removed, but she couldn't get away from the pain of looking at it every day, being reminded of the one person who'd loved her enough to listen to whatever she would say.

Another trip to the stream to calm herself down drives her off her feet.

She resists the water, its reflection showing that her true age has returned.

The old woman must be decades older now, she thinks to herself.

Returning to the woman's lodging, she finds a pile of bones and is glad to not have witnessed this scene, too. An animal by the door gives her a nod, somehow telling her to turn around. She spins and takes a step forward, and the grass beneath her swallows her whole.

Finding this feeling familiar and comforting, she does not resist. She says her goodbyes, and tells her best friend that she still loves her. The passageway carrying her up narrows in a little, as if to hug her, and releases itself back to its normal shape. As if she's about to approach a handlebar she needs to grab on to, she reaches up and notices the tattoo sparkling with new life. She takes a fetal position, her eyelids swim closed and she appears to be reborn.

A cool night breeze sends her hair flying and she unbuckles her knees from her chest to find herself seated on some steps across her favorite coffee shop, the one she spends most mornings in, watching people walk by.

Stretching her legs to stand up, the man in the trench coat exits the coffee shop with two drinks in hand.

"Sheila!" he calls.

She feels lightheaded, the blood in her head rushing to anywhere but where it's supposed to be. She feels naked almost. No. That's not right; she feels *seen*.

She had met him at one of those work trainings, he seemed normal, boring, average. At the end of the training, he'd suggested everyone get drinks at the virtual reality bar down the street. She had gone and he had charmed her quite a bit, speaking of literature she liked and sites she adored. He had made her feel special, had given all his attention to her, but at the end of the night, his girlfriend had joined him. She felt that she always got her hopes up way too high.

She'd left the function wondering how many other people she'd connect with, but not fully be able to know.

The sky fills with sparkling stars, all seeming to wink at her with motions of grandeur life.

He apologizes for taking so long, "There was a line."

He hands her a tea and offers his arm, saying he regrets coming on so strong when they'd first met, saying that he'd felt stifled in his previous relationship, saying he's grateful for another chance to get to know her. She reaches up to take the cup and something catches his eye.

"Is that a new tattoo?" he asks.

"New in the sense that I've kept it hidden all this time," she says.

Just like every other detail of her life.

She'd never spoken of her loss, or of any other affairs. But she sees now—how coming to terms with pains of the past opens up a new way of seeing. One in which the stars glimmer with hope, butterflies long for human connection, and everyone else is just another person, trying to figure everything out.

Mahaprasthanika (The Great Journey)

By

Monica Singh

A firefly fluttered across the dark expanse in luxurious, giddy circles, leaving a trail of glow dust in its wake. Soon, a thicket of sal trees swallowed the momentary glimmer as night resumed its shadowy prowl.

Devavrat watched the firefly from a roughly ploughed hole in the earth. Oddly, it comforted him. Darkness was a slave of the littlest spark of light, but a flicker of darkness as inconsequential as a firefly could never hope to obliterate light.

He heaved a sigh and turned over. The canopy of snakelike branches overhead obscured the sky completely. The night was pregnant with the cricket's song, and yonder, a faint tinkling of bells cut through the cacophony of the sleeping forest sending shivers of incomprehensible dread down his spine.

Unbidden, the fear and exhaustion of the day caught up with him in a rising tide of grief and shock. He curled into a ball and bit his lips to suppress the howl of pain that threatened to overpower him. Tears cascaded down his cheeks as flashes of the nightmare he had witnessed pushed aside every other thought, clamouring for his attention.

"Please let them be safe," he whispered to the night. "Please."

Savdhaan! Aakraman!

The battle cries shattered the calm that had enveloped the Aryabani settlement just moments ago.

"Deva! They are here!"

His mother's voice cut through the thick veil of sleep. Devavrat grunted and blinked awake. The dusk was imbued with an unnatural orange hue. Red and gold flared across his blurred vision.

He sat bolt upright. His mother, Ambakaruni, retrieved a spear from their small armoury. The jagged triangle of flint at its end glinted dangerously.

"We are under attack, Deva!" she said. "They are here. You must go, now!"

Deva stared, befuddled.

Ambakaruni had discarded her decorous robes of white cotton, indicative of her stature as the tribe's chieftain, in favour of the plain leatherette combat gear. Dark brown trousers coupled with a half-tunic served the dual purpose of covering her bodice and acting as a shield against stray arrows and sword jabs. Her silvery hair was held in place with a black bandana. She looked nothing like her fifty years demanded.

Amba cupped Deva's face in her free hand.

"We are out of time. You know what needs to be done. You must go to the *shriban*."

Deva rose, swatting her hand away, and hurriedly strapped on his leather vestments.

"No, mother. I am needed here."

He grabbed his spear and made towards the door, but Amba stood resolutely in his way.

"There's nothing here for you. Vanarban calls you."

"There's nothing in Vanarban for me! Nothing!"

Twin drops of saline dew escaped Amba's brown eyes as she regarded her only son.

"You will do as you are told, Devavrat. This might be…." her voice trembled with emotion, "this might be the last thing I ask of you."

"Mother!"

She pointed her spear at him, "You *will* obey me. If not as a request from your mother, then as a command from your Chief! You have hidden from your destiny long enough."

Deva stood dumbfounded. Juxtaposed against the backdrop of the fiery carnage outside, she looked divine; not a woman, but a force. A personified sliver of that much-rumoured Goddess Shakti itself.

"C… come with me," he said, his words carrying the beseeching wail of a child calling to his mother for comfort, "we can both go..."

Instantly, he knew he had said the wrong thing. The sudden transformation of her features frightened him.

"I hope to the Gods that I did not raise a coward! The last remaining seed of my beloved, Siddhartha, a coward?" She turned away from him. "Begone! Return to us when you have grown into the man you were meant to be. Or perish trying. May the Gods be with you, Deva."

She gave him a last, wistful glance and then determinedly walked through the doors.

🌲 🌲 🌲

"*Ma…*!"

Deva startled awake. He opened his eyes, and the world rushed in. Golden sunlight filtered through the canopy of the trees above.

Another day. It's another day.

He breathed deeply and the scents of the wild pervaded his nostrils. The petrichor of wet earth mingled with the sweet odour of vegetation and the unmistakable musk of wet fur and manure. The chirping of songbirds was so loud, Deva wondered how he had slept through all the racket.

As he unfurled his coiled limbs, his entire body protested in a hodgepodge of popping joints and screaming tendons. He clambered out of his makeshift shelter and worked out the kinks with determined single-mindedness.

I am here, mother. He angrily massaged his calf muscles. *Much good it has done me.*

Mud caked his lower legs. He whispered a silent prayer of thanks for the leather-soled sandals he had remembered to wear before leaving his hut.

Sneaking from the hut, he corrected. *Like a thief in the night. Coward!*

Instantly, the anger seeped out of him. His hands fell at his sides as he gazed around himself, unseeing.

He didn't know how long he sat there, wallowing in self-pity and lost in the memories of a life that had abandoned him until a loud rumbling from his belly alerted him of his hunger.

When was the last time I ate? He couldn't remember. *Water. I need water. To drink and wash.*

Deva had heard the tale of a freshwater stream that flowed from the far-off mountains and enriched the Vanarban basin. While he had seen no hide nor hair of the stream, generations of Aryabani hunters swore about its existence deep in the forest.

He sighed. Since leaving the settlement, he had followed the hunter's path through the forest. Now, a day into the wild depths, the well-trodden trail was already fading. He couldn't rely on it any longer. Picking up his spear, he walked on.

No Aryabani had dared come this far inside Vanarban, at least none alive. His father had made the journey once, but the merciless life-cycle of the forest had wiped away any traces of his passing.

Located on a small pocket of flatland, on the very outskirts of the Kingdom of Gandharpur; the ever-impenetrable depths of Vanarban surrounded the Aryabani settlement on three sides. Only a roughly hewn footpath connected their small hold to the city.

Their tribe was so removed from civilization that the city dwellers perceived the Aryabani to be the spirits of Vanarban. Their isolation fueled the rumours; notwithstanding that theirs was one of the very last tribes of its kind that still clung to the old beliefs and the dying Gods.

It had been these very beliefs that had led Siddhartha to the depths of the *shriban*, in search of… something.

Deva staggered through the undergrowth towards a patch of sky where birds flew in a cacophonous flurry.

Where there are birds, there's water.

The legends surrounding Vanarban had never made sense to him. Deva had grown up listening to the horror stories of the tribesmen who had wandered off the beaten path and never returned. Whatever secrets the forest held, none of the Aryabani men had uncovered them.

None except father. How did he survive when better hunters and warriors failed? Do divine spirits truly roam here? And if they do, why would they take others while letting his father go?

The light reflecting off the gleaming surface of a small lake broke his reverie. He hurried over the grassy knoll and presently stood at the edge of a marshy depression with the lake at its centre. His relief was palpable. *It was real, after all.*

He clambered down, his thirst a searing, insistent need. Dropping to the wet, muddy bank, he let his spear fall beside him. He was about to lower his face into the water when his reflection distracted him. The face staring back at him was shockingly alien. Dark shoulder length hair lay lank around his drawn face.

Scratches ran the length of his cheeks, blood scabbing over the deeper ones. The eyes that peered out from behind that gaunt, haunted face seemed dead. A husk of the boy who used to be Devavrat.

He punched a fist through the surface, and the image scattered. Cupping the clear water in his hands, he brought them to his parched lips, but paused. A tinkling of bells. He was sure he had heard it last night in his dazed sleep, too. Unnerved, he looked around. What was its source? Droplets of water escaped down his hands and left him cupping only air in his palms.

Deva blinked, and there she was! A girl, walking serenely along the opposite side of the lake like an apparition. The tinkling came from her; with every step, her anklets rang with a musical jingling of nubile happiness. She was like a child; and yet, there was something so overwhelmingly alluring about her that he couldn't take his eyes off her. Presently, the girl stepped into the lake. Her graceful shoulders and bejewelled ankles gleamed in the sun. She looked at him, and a tingle ran up his spine.

Paransavi? he thought, astounded. She looked like his betrothed back at home. *No. Savi couldn't be here.*

The girl smiled, her green eyes crinkling, and the forest seemed to smile with her.

"I am not the one you search for, traveller."

Her voice was a melodious symphony of the very force that made up Vanarban.

Whispers of some long-forgotten tales from his childhood rushed through the fog of grief and shock.

Aranyani? Was she the Goddess of the forest? The divine energy that kept the forest alive? Dancing in the wake of tinkling anklets?

"I have many names," she said, as if she was aware of the thoughts racing through Deva's mind. "None of them are wrong; none of them entirely correct either."

Even as Deva struggled to comprehend, her voice cut through his thoughts.

"You have come at a crossroads, Devavrat. This stream divides your path in two. One leads you in your father's footsteps, through the depths of this jungle. The other, to death."

She smiled, her eyes glittering with a different, darker energy now.

"If you ask me, the path to death is the simpler one. One drink from the lake," she indicated the clear blue water, "I know you want to."

A note of seductive enticement entered her voice. The urge to drink was overpowering. He was so thirsty, as if he had not had a drop of water ever in his life.

"What…," he croaked, his voice raspy and painful against his dry throat, "what is the other path?"

Aranyani's features clouded.

"If you wish to proceed, you cannot drink from the lake. You must turn towards the *shriban, the Sacred Grove*. The journey will be fraught with dangers from the wildren. I cannot estimate the length or difficulty of the journey ahead, but I am certain you will arrive at your destination. How you exploit the opportunity is entirely your choice."

Deva stared at her, nonplussed. *What sort of crossroads was this?* As far as he could see, there was nothing but pain and death.

Do I want to go on?

He stared longingly at the water, and his heart screamed in anguish. If only he could drink a little. Just a small sip of the cool water so he could think.

"I can take away your pain, Devavrat," Aranyani murmured, lulling him in a strange cocoon of warmth. "Just one sip and this pointless suffering will be over."

Deva agreed. It was pointless. Out there, his people were being butchered, and he was here, all alone, defenceless. *Useless.*

"Useless!" Paransavi folded her hands across her chest in disapproval.

"It's so cumbersome and uncomfortable!" Devavrat whined.

The Chief's headdress was an exaggeratedly large circlet of interwoven pieces of sticks, animal bones, and straw. He had been itching to try on the headdress for ages, and with his mother out hunting, this evening had presented him with the perfect opportunity.

Besides, it wasn't as if she could complain. It belonged to him now.

"They make crowns to be cumbersome and uncomfortable, Deva," Savi said scathingly. "It is unbecoming of a Chief to show his displeasure of it. It's a symbol of responsibility and pride, to be borne with dignity. Besides, you shouldn't even be wearing it before the tribe raises you as Chief!"

Deva waved a hand in dismissal. "But, I am going to be Chief soon enough!"

Paransavi shook her head. "Sometimes, you are such a child, Deva."

Deva grunted his disagreement, but prudently kept silent. Savi was as quick with words as she was with her spear. Only a fool would engage her in an argument, and Deva was no fool.

She tucked a stray lock of dark hair behind a small, tender ear. The leather combat tunic and trousers seemed to be a second skin on her wiry frame. Not for her the frivolities of flowered skirts and beaded necklaces. No. She was born to be a hunter. The only accessory to her otherwise drab outfit was the yellow bandana she wore to contain her waist-length hair. The contrast of her bronze skin with the yellow so pleasing that Deva's heart gave an odd sort of flutter.

"Did you hear about the attack on Kamathipura?" she asked, conspiratorially, her eyes wide. "They executed the Royal Family! Entire city is in ashes! Some hunters came across a caravan of refugees the other day. They claim the plunderers are a godless lot. Not satisfied with the killing, they even bludgeoned the temples to the ground. Desecrating holy places with blood!" she trembled.

"Deva, do you think they will attack us?"

He lowered the headdress to the floor and swept back his tousled hair.

"They haven't attacked Gandharpur yet, and it's the closest city to us. Who would want to plunder a band of nobodies when there are treasures to be had in Gandharpur?"

"But, didn't you notice how worried the elders are? It's not all about the riches. These invaders want to wipe out every vestige of our way of life. Our heritage and our Gods! They want to spread their barbaric notions of faith. They say that *we* are the traitors."

She jutted her chin out, a gesture of defiance.

"I think if there's even a possibility of attack, we should prepare to fight."

Deva sighed. "You sound just like my mother. There is no fighting with these people, Savi. I think the best defence is to leave here before the plunderers come calling."

"That's the coward's way out! Besides, where are we to go? This is our home!" Paransavi shook her head, bewildered.

Deva stood up, his fists balling in anger. He was no coward! It wasn't his fault that neither his mother nor his betrothed would listen to reason.

"If the might of Kamathipura couldn't stop these invaders, you really think we stand a chance?" he asked. "If we don't run away, they will slaughter us like animals!"

Savi rose, glaring. The affection in her eyes transformed into contempt.

"How dare you? We are Aryabani! We do not run!"

You are foolish, he thought as he turned away and struggled to pull the ceremonial robes over his head.

Savi let out a disdainful snort. "If only you could inherit sense and respect like you inherit the crown, Deva. You have to earn it. Like your father. And you know what is to be done."

"I am not going into the forest on a fool's quest," he muttered, unwilling to look at her.

He could feel the disappointment radiating off her.

"You are setting yourself up for certain failure. This is your responsibility as the heir of the last Chief. You had better grow into it!"

My responsibility, he thought.

He opened his eyes. To his surprise, he was still crouched beside the lake. Aranyani tilted her head, a question in her eyes.

"I…" Deva scooted away from her, reluctantly shaking off the residue of water from his hands. "I wish to proceed."

Aranyani said nothing, only sighed, her expression softening. She smiled, and this time, Deva felt its warm, healing embrace.

"Your father's spirit guides you, even if your purpose eludes you. Go with my blessing. May you find what you seek."

Deva blinked, and Aranyani was gone.

When Deva woke up next, it was dark. The lake was nowhere in sight. He lay under a copse of trees in a different part of the forest.

How did I come here? When did I come here?

Try as he might, all he could remember was Aranyani's smiling face. He sat up, and to his bewildering relief, his body didn't scream in pain. The various aches that had homed in on him ever since he had started his journey seemed to have vanished. He felt energised, almost healed.

Did Aranyani do this?

He lay back, thinking. In hindsight, Deva couldn't fathom the reasons for his choice. Aranyani hadn't been lying when she said that death was the simpler route. So, why had he been unwilling for that release? Was it guilt? Regret? Or was it some foolish notion of seeking redemption through self-immolation?

He closed his eyes. Whatever the reason, the choice was made. Now he had to follow through. He hoped he was strong enough for whatever lay ahead.

Deva leaned against the thick trunk of a sagun tree to catch his breath. He had lost count of the number of days he had spent wandering through the wild after his meeting with Aranyani. Amid the constantly unforgiving landscape, the only sign of the passage of time had been the rising and setting of the sun. The strength gained after his encounter with the forest goddess had leached out of him. Now, he was weary of mind and body. His leather tunic lay in tatters, his skin torn apart with innumerable scratches earned as he hacked his way through the underbrush.

His left leg smarted painfully. The wound below his knee was an agonising, festering reminder of a close encounter with a ravenous wild boar. He had wrapped it up in a crude splint of sticks and leaves. Under the circumstances, it was the best solution.

A strange screeching broke his train of thought and Deva stumbled a few paces forwards till he stood in the shadows behind the treeline. What he saw made him stare transfixed.

Monkeys!

There were hundreds of them! Their movements rippled in a seething mass of brown, like waves in an ocean. Some hopped and jumped over one another, some reclined, apparently sleeping. Some fussed over infants that clung to their mothers while others prowled around the flock like guardians. A few even languished in the branches of the nearby *sthalavriksha*. The air was rife with their chittering; the noise overwhelming the sounds of the forest.

Is this the place? Am I here at last?

The structure that served as the monkeys' lair was an old ruin at the very centre of the clearing. Through the gaps between the mass of furry limbs and vivid red bottoms, jagged, age-blackened stones peeped out. Two stone steps led the way to a raised platform. On either side of what must have once been an arched gopuram, stood two pillars covered with trailing vines and leaves. A collection of upright walls gave the impression of spacious chambers. Nothing remained of the pinnacle, which must have caved in over the years.

The pile of rubble scattered around the structure was all that remained of the temple's original architecture.

Deva's heartbeat rose to a crescendo. *Go inside*, it urged him.

Hesitation bounded his feet. Daylight was fading. The monkeys didn't look threatening, but if they perceived him as a threat, they would attack.

"A misstep in the dark can end your life in Vanarban," he whispered the age-old saying of his people to the resolutely indifferent *sagun* tree.

Deva decided to make camp for the night. He quickly collected some dead branches and leaves for a fire and retreated to a depression in the ground. The undergrowth was blessedly dry, and the fire caught with little effort. He kept it small for fear of attracting unwanted attention. One could never be sure what hid in the depths of Vanarban.

He had caught a rabbit earlier in the day and he unwrapped the hank of dried meat from his waistband, placing it on the hot rocks beside the fire. Not the best of provisions, but it would keep him alive. He settled down, watching the crackling fire, smelling the cooking meat.

The tiny fire reminded him of a different fireside; vibrant flashes of a boy running around the nightly campfire, shrieking with giddy pleasure. It was a wonder how that boy had survived in this interminable wilderness. But he had. He was finally here. Sore and exhausted, but very much alive.

"Once I have fulfilled my duty within the temple, I will return home," he told the fire. *Home.* The word felt alien on his tongue. Like a place from someone else's memories.

A soft rustling broke his ruminations. Instantly alert, he grabbed his spear and crouched low, ready to jump, eyes fruitlessly peering through the darkness. His body erupted in gooseflesh as a sudden chill swooped down his spine and clutched at his heart.

A man stood in the darkness dressed in a similar combat gear, only darker, more frayed. The tunic and the trousers weren't intertwined with twigs and leaves, rather they were woven with them. Long, silvery hair lay strewn about on his shoulders in matted dreadlocks. He was taller than Deva by a head, but slender, more wiry. Even though the stranger's entire body was covered in dust, his dark eyes shone bright.

An ambush? No, it's a spectre! his mind screamed at him. One of the forest spirits. Why else had I not heard him approach?

"Greetings, Chief," the man said, bowing his head, his voice was like the rumbling of mountains. "I have a long road ahead and no source of respite. Might I share your fire?"

"I am not a Chief," Deva said warily.

"Then, I pray you will soon come to great honour," the man said. "I am Vyas. You can lower your virginal spear, child. I come in peace."

Suddenly, Deva felt like an utter fool. The man was weapon-less and ancient. The firelight cast deep shadows across the wrinkled chasms of his face. A wooden staff held precariously in his right hand was probably the only thing supporting his stance.

"Please, join me."

The man stepped out of the shadows, or rather, the shadows retreated behind him as he stepped towards the fire and settled down. He laid the staff by his side and gratefully extended his hands to the warmth of the fire.

"It's an unexpected pleasure meeting a fellow in these parts," he said, regarding Deva with undivided scrutiny. "Tell me, what brings you here?"

"I could ask you the same thing," Deva said with a hint of defiance. "Where do you come from?"

"Yes, I am far from my abode," the old man said, his features betraying a hint of wistfulness. "Or, perhaps, not at all. You must forgive me, it's not for me to divine a truth where none exists."

What kind of answer was that?

Vyas stoked the fire with a stick, and it rose in a spiral of merry sparks. A comforting warmth spread through Deva's being. There was something about this man that gave him pause.

Who is he? Why is he here? Is his presence, on the very eve of the culmination of my journey, a sign from the divine? But then what about the temple? Am I not supposed to go inside?

"You look like one of those Aryabani men." Vyas's words penetrated the deep fog of Deva's thoughts. "I am surprised. I dare say your lot do not venture into the forest often."

"No, we don't," Deva said, intrigue rising.

If this man knew about their settlement, could he also know of their current whereabouts?

"Have you been there recently?" he asked, unable to contain the plea in his voice.

"No," Vyas shook his head, "but, I heard about the attack. Nothing left there, but ash and dust. The faithless believe that death is too convenient a way to escape the humiliation of conquest. They took many prisoners. Those that died, died with honour."

Deva stifled a grimace, unwilling to let out the pain he held captive inside him. Suddenly, he wanted to be left alone. He wished the old man would just get up and leave.

Ah! To have the freedom of wallowing in my guilt and let the regret drown me into the void of nothingness!

"You look troubled, child," Vyas said kindly.

"I was there when the savages attacked," Deva murmured, his voice barely a whisper above the crackling of the fire.

"My mother, she… she forced me to come here while she stayed behind to fight. I told them to run. *I told them* we couldn't possibly stand against their might, but they wouldn't listen to me!"

He was weeping now, and he found he didn't care.

"You call them faithless, but what use is having faith when it doesn't come to your rescue when you need it? The Aryabani have been faithful for centuries. What did that bring us? Poverty, squalor and filth. We stayed true to our faith. Look what happened to us!" Deva said, spreading his hands in a gesture of debilitating defeat as tears streamed down his cheeks unchecked.

"When *Kaal* came knocking, our Gods could not even protect themselves. How are they supposed to protect us? Those that you call the faithless rule the nation and the faithful lie gathering dust." All the anger he had bottled up in some forgotten part of his mind came rushing out like a flood.

Uncharacteristically, Vyas smiled.

"The idols in your temple are not Gods. Stone isn't God. It's your faith that makes stones worthy of worship. The Divine is infinite, Devavrat. It lives in that stone just as much as it lives within us. Yes, the idols you worship cannot protect you. They cannot take up arms against your enemies, but you can."

"At what cost? You cannot fight if you are dead. There is no honour in *death*!"

Deva spat into the fire.

"You do not believe that defending your homeland is honourable?" Vyas asked with unflinching resolve.

"The place that gave you life, the elements that course through your veins, the culture and the faith that keeps your tribe together isn't worth defending?"

Deva shook his head. "We could have gone somewhere else. Safe from them. Then, maybe we would have had enough time to prepare…"

"And when is that? How much time is enough time? What will happen until the time you are prepared to take up arms to protect those you love and the very elements that make you? Would you prefer a life of humiliation and shame? Is it honourable to live devoid of will and purpose, or to die knowing that you served the divine in the best way you knew how? We call them faithless, but you and I both know that they have lost much more than just their faith. At least they are driven by their desires, however corrupt they might be."

Vyas pointed a gnarled finger at the silhouette of the ruined temple in the distance.

"Why are you here, Devavrat? What drives you?"

Deva reeled in the echoing silence that followed. The old man hadn't raised his voice, but Deva felt like his words had slapped him awake. The haze of fear, the interminable dejection and disillusionment he had carried with him throughout his life, seemed to lift, making way for a sliver of light.

"I… I don't know," he mumbled and realised that for the first time since he had stepped inside Vanarban, he was telling himself the truth.

Vyas smiled, eyes lighting up with an indescribable, unadulterated joy.

"Then, I suggest you find out. And, soon. It's nearly time now, Devavrat. You are nearly there."

Abruptly, Vyas bid him a good night and laid down next to the fire. Soon, the soft vibrations of his snoring joined the melee of the forest.

But sleep evaded Deva. He sat beside the fire thinking over everything Vyas had said.

Why was I here? If I truly believed that nothing could be gained from the Gods, or my faith, why had I trodden through this vast wilderness, struggling to survive just one more day? Why hadn't I laid down in a ditch somewhere, allowing the wildren to chew off my flesh? Why had I not allowed Aranyani to end my misery?

His mother's last command rang across the distance separating them. *Return to us when you have grown into the man you were meant to be. Or perish trying.*

By the time Deva laid down and slipped into a dreamless sleep, the fire had died down to smouldering embers. When morning came, Vyas was nowhere to be seen.

Deva took a deep breath and limped towards the ruins; head lowered to avoid the many brown eyes following his progress.

"I want to go inside," he chanted like a mantra. "I don't mean any harm."

Some part of him wondered how he would make his intentions clear to the monkeys.

He had already covered half the distance to the temple when he noticed the deafening silence around him. Yesterday, the place echoed with the monkeys' screeches. Today, the air reverberated with the quiet of a graveyard. Against his better judgement, he looked up. The animals were staring at him.

Disconcerted, he took a few steps backwards, tripping on his wounded leg. He prayed the fierce trembling of his limbs would stop. The monkeys maintained their silent vigil.

Is this a test? Do I have to get past this army of apes? How had father dealt with them? Why did I never ask him?

There were too many to fight. Violence wouldn't work here. What other alternative did he have? This derelict ruin is their home. They aren't going to move aside and let him waltz in. Abruptly, the truth of his thoughts struck him.

Of course!

If these mute animals knew enough to stand and fight for their home, how could he ever blame his people for wishing to do the same?

Muffling the anguished scream that rose within him, he gazed at the apes and understood what he had to do. He stood up and approached the ruin. Stopping just before the crumbling stone steps, he folded his hands and bowed.

"I come to partake of the divine blessing that was given to my father and his father before him. I come seeking wisdom. I don't mean to harm your tribe. I only wish to find some means to save mine. If I am not w…," Deva's voice cracked under the burden of the eventuality he did not want to consider.

He breathed deeply and tried again. "If I am not worthy, give me a sign and I will leave."

He opened his eyes and looked expectantly at the sea of blinking brown. Had they understood him? He clasped his trembling fingers tightly, afraid to let go.

Suddenly, the troop of monkeys sitting in the central courtyard of the temple rose and walked away, clearing a path to the garbhagriha.

Deva sighed, his limbs uncoiling, releasing the breath with a whoosh. He climbed the steps and stood inside the courtyard for a moment.

I am one of them now, Deva thought and murmured a prayer of thanks to the Gods.

🌲 🌲 🌲

At the very centre of the temple, another set of stone steps led the way to an underground chamber. Gingerly, Deva made his way down to the *garbhagriha.* In the temples at home, it contained the dais bearing stone idols of the deities.

But the space he emerged into resembled a small cellar. Being underground, this chamber was protected from the elements. To his surprise, rather than the rank odour of enclosed, abandoned places, the air inside was suffused with a pleasant, flowery aroma. It was clean and light and empty.

Deva frowned. Where was the dais? The idols? His perplexed gaze swept through the chamber again and landed on a small pool of water in a far corner. He hurried towards it. Kneeling beside the pool, he examined the chamber again; nothing else there except this pool.

Remarkably, the water was a clear blue. Leaning forward, he could see his reflection staring back at him. It reminded him of his encounter with Aranyani, but this place had a different energy.

In the centre of the pool was a large mound of black stone. A lingam. Hesitatingly, he reached out and laid his fingers on the slick, wet surface. It was about waist height and a foot thick; smooth and round. Shapeless. Formless. His fingertips caressed the stone's surface, and he felt a powerful aura emanate from it. It seemed alive. Humming with an intense, contained energy.

There was an awareness in it that sent a shiver down his spine.

Am I touching the stone, or is it touching me?

He breathed sharply and closed his eyes, allowing the strange sensation to envelop him. It felt like he was falling face forward into the pool. A sense of indeterminate weightlessness came over him.

An old man leaned over the same pool where Deva had been just seconds before. Dressed in the ceremonial attire of the Aryabani Chief, he looked more like a King, his features set in grim determination.

Have I travelled elsewhere?

Disconcerted, Deva stared around and, to his astonishment, the temple had transformed. Chamber walls, studded with precious gems. The vimana, decorated with carved motifs, rising heavenward with flighty perseverance. The pool itself sparkled under the beams of brilliant sunlight filtering in through the colourful window panes along the ceiling.

Then, a flurry of colours. Another man lay howling beside the pool. The temple had changed. It was less glorious, faded. The motifs were ragged and window panes cracked.

Why had nobody bothered to fix them?

Deva was then transported to the presence of another man. This one, he recognised instantly. The Elder Chief, his grandsire, with an expression of dejection on his face. The temple inched steadily towards inevitable ruination.

His heart beat faster, blood pumped in his ears. Now, he was eager to see. Anticipation made him break out in a cold sweat. He knew what was coming next. *Who* was coming next. The world blurred, and when the shadows retreated,

Deva saw his father, the previous and last rightful Chief of his people sitting beside the pool.

Appa...!

His knees buckled, and he dropped to the floor beside his father. He wanted to reach out and touch him, go to him.

Oh, to be loved again, to be safe again! Just for a moment.

What wouldn't he give to have the opportunity of hearing his comforting rumble of a voice sweep over him one last time.

Why did you leave me?! his heart cried out, beseeching the apparition to atone for the abandonment. *Why, Appa? Why did you leave this burden on my shoulders? I am not worthy!*

His father stood up and glanced around the now crumbling structure. For a moment, his sorrowful eyes rested on the spot where Deva sat, howling and moaning. Then, he squared his shoulders, a deep breath of relief and a small smile of purpose realised. Then, he was gone.

The vision faded, and the world was enveloped, once again, in the swishing of winds.

Deva plunged headfirst amid the battle that had raged in his settlement. The night was painted orange and red. Deva's mother was in close combat with a man who seemed to be the leader of the invading savages. Over at the other side, a group of hunters battled on, with enemy soldiers bent on approaching their temple. Deva saw a glimpse of an achingly familiar yellow bandana that vanished in the melee. He was flying away to a different place.

He stood amidst a burning settlement. A different one, but he could see hints of familiar eyes and noses. The

carnage was astounding. Bodies covered the ground.
Firelight reflected darkly off the accumulated pools of blood.
In the mass of the dead and dying, a single man stood facing
the retreating army in the distance. He aided those who could
be helped, dragging the injured to one side. And the dead to
the other.

"We mustn't lose hope," he kept repeating to the
glassy-eyed populace.

"Look around you, Kesava!" another voice rose from the
mass. "There's nothing left. They destroyed everything!"

"We are going to make it through," the man said. "We
will rebuild and we will keep fighting! We are the Aryabani!
As long as we are together."

"There's nothing left of the Aryabani. They will come
again, and there is nothing we can do to stop them. If we are
to survive, we must leave here."

Deva left the man standing, bereft of hope, watching
helplessly as his people left him behind like the useless
detritus of their lives.

Now, he was with the invaders. Attacking the hapless
remnants of a tribe that seemed to have retreated deeper into
Vanarban. The ruins of the temple rested forlornly in the
distance, like a mound of useless rubble covered by weeds.

There were no more monkeys now. The forest itself
seemed dead. Lifeless.

He gazed at it with sorrowful repentance.

We couldn't save it.

A group of soldiers approached the ruins with
sledgehammers and battle axes. With a pang of shock, Deva
saw his own features reflected in the man who led the
invaders. Deva and his troops descended upon the ruins with
a surge of black hatred, destroying the weed-covered walls

and eventually the garbhagriha, where Deva could still see the clear pond of blue water.

No!

With a mighty effort of will, Deva prised his fingers off the lingam and lurched back to his reality. He rolled across the floor and screamed until his throat hurt.

Anguished tears bled out from his eyes. Surely, there could be no shame in crying now. He realised with a tragic certainty that he had just witnessed the ultimate demise of his people. The horrifying truth of their future. It took a long time for his sobs to subside.

The sky overhead was dark. He was exhausted; breathing in painful bursts.

"Is this our destiny? Is this why you called me here? To show me how we are all doomed?" he asked the stone.

There was no answer.

Suddenly, Deva wished he had never come here. That man had looked exactly like him. Why was he fighting with the savages? Why did the Aryabani lose their battle spirit? When did they become runaways? Was he to blame for it?

It didn't occur to him to deny the evidence of his eyes. This was the truth. He was certain of it. This wasn't the fear of a crazed God or spirit taking the form of vision or possibilities.

No, these events were real. This would happen. Slowly, but surely, the Aryabani were headed towards their destruction.

"Can I change it?" he asked, closing his eyes.

If I can't, will that stop me from trying?

No. It was as simple as that. How could he live with himself knowing that he could have averted the terrible fate that awaited his people?

He opened his eyes and gritted his teeth. The Aryabani weren't cowards. They fought for their honour. If he was the only one who knew the terrors of their future, then it was his duty to act. His mother's parting words came to him again like a divine prophecy.

I will be worthy, Mother. I will be worthy, or I will die trying.

He turned away from the pool. The darkness outside was absolute, but never had his path been so clear. He climbed out of the garbhagriha and into the night, breaking into an ungainly run. He had to return. He had to go home. His people called to him. His duty called to him.

Glossary:

Aakraman: Attack.

Appa: Father.

Aranyani Devi: The goddess of forests; the guardian deity of sacred sanctuaries, woodlands and jungles.

Garbhagriha: The sanctum sanctorum, the innermost sanctuary of a Hindu and Jain temples where resides the murti (idol or icon) of the primary deity of the temple.

Gopuram: A monumental entrance tower, usually ornate, at the entrance of a Hindu temple.

Kalasha: The topmost pinnacle of the temple.

Lingam: A symbol of divine generative energy, especially a phallus or phallic object as a symbol of Shiva. Sometimes referred to as linga, or Shiva linga, is an abstract or aniconic representation of the Hindu god Shiva in Shaivism. It is typically the primary murti or devotional image in Hindu temples dedicated to Shiva, also found in smaller shrines, or as self-manifested natural objects

Ma: Mother.

Sagun: Teak tree.

Savdhaan: Attention.

Shakti: The female principle of divine energy, especially when personified as the supreme deity.

Shriban: Sacred Grove.

Sthalavriksha: A monumental tree that is indigenous to every historical Hindu temple.

Vanarban: Vanar - (Hindi) monkey; ban - (Hindi) forest.

Vimana: The tallest structure of the temple over the inner sanctum.

DISCLAIMER, REFERENCES AND ATTRIBUTIONS:

Mahaprasthanika Parva (Sanskrit: महाप्रस्थानिक पर्व), or the "Book of the Great Journey," is the seventeenth of eighteen books of the Indian Puranic epic *Mahabharata.* It recites the journey of the Pandavas across India and their ascent towards Himalayas as they climb their way to heaven on Mount Sumeru.

This is a work of fiction set in a period of Indian history when *Aranya* (forests) played a central role in human life and spiritual development. Forests were seen as *shri bhumi* (sacred land), ruled by nature, the wildlings and other mysterious laws that were beyond human comprehension. Many Indian temples have a close relationship with forests and most Gods are believed to be associated with particular plants, trees, flowers, fruits, seeds and other forms of flora. In India, there are over 15,000 well-documented sacred groves. They are divided into *tapovan* (forests for sages and ascetics to offer penance), *mahavan* (jungle sanctuaries), and *shriban* (sacred groves).

Devavrat's journey begins at a time when the grand *Jambudvipa* (Bharatvarsha or The Grand Undivided India) was being invaded by pockets of foreign attackers. This story attempts to describe a sliver of the struggle of the indeginous residents to safeguard their homes, cultures and their very existence.

The names of the characters and places in this story have been inspired from the Epic *Mahabharata*. However, unless otherwise indicated, all the names, characters, businesses, places, events and incidents in this book are either the product of the author's imagination or used in a fictitious manner. Any resemblance to actual persons, living or dead, or actual events is purely coincidental.

The Lionfish Flower

By

Keanu Joaquin Del Toro

*D*on't get me wrong, I love my succulents, but I kinda want something to brag about.

Catalina sends the text to her friend Yolanda, and locks the door to her house. Garbage bag in hand, she lifts the lid of the trash bin and a raccoon hisses and leaps from its makeshift lair. Catalina shrieks and flails as the critter hops the fence to her backyard and dashes for the trees and long browning grass.

"Goddamn trash panda," she says, tossing the bag in the bin and ducking into her car, a Toyota Camry that's just under drinking age. She slides her phone into her back pocket.

Today is the sunniest it's been all week, no thanks to the tropical storms that have washed the town in gray since June. On this Monday afternoon, what feels like the slowest day of August, is itself the calm before the storm—the university preparing for the oncoming student body to make its grand return to campus life. If it weren't for the usual traffic and honking every afternoon, one would think it's been a ghost town.

The heat buzzes with intense concentration. Everything is too bright, even her dirty sad tofu gray car with its brown undertone has a high albedo. Through her squinting, Catalina manages to unlock her car and dons her shades, tinted blue with round square lenses to emphasize their tackiness.

"Everything is sexier through shades," she says to no one in particular.

The farmer's market bakes in the summer haze; a couple tables shaded with tents and umbrellas all lay bare to the sun. After only a few yards into her short walk, Catalina builds a bead of sweat on her brow.

The tables flank a gazebo, housing jars of honey, jam, fruit preserves, a rack of healthy snack bars and other vegan-life curiosities. The aromatic ambience is countered by the stench of grass and the sweaty souls who have previously attended the booths.

Yolanda emerges from behind her table, greeting her friend while dabbing sweat from her forehead. She's wearing her uniform, a simple graphic tee with the company logo of a potted plant and *GreenWaze* in black printed across a field of green.

"Hey, Cat! You're up early," Yolanda says with her chipper and sweet voice.

"Yeah, I know, it's only two o'clock," Cat follows with a flimsy laugh.

They give each other a quick hug, Yolanda's shirt sticking to her skin. She gathers her afro into a bun and heads to her table.

"Damn, it's hot," Cat follows and ties her hair into a short ponytail. "How do you guys deal with this?"

"Well, a lot of patience, love, and homemade lemonade iced tea. Say that three times fast."

Yolanda pours a cup for her and Cat thanks her.

"The whole thing or just the last part?" Cat eyes the fruit gummies as she sips.

"Now I wanna hear you say the whole thing."

"Homelaid—ugh."

Yolanda chuckles.

"You can sit with me," she gestures to a beach chair next to her own.

"Sounds good, I want some gummies," Catalina says as she digs through her handbag for her wallet.

"Which flavor?"

"Mango Lychee Ouija Board. That sounds insane."

She pays for the snack and plops herself down, taking a quick glance around.

"Where's everyone else?"

"I don't know," Yolanda leans back in her chair. "They haven't gotten back to us yet. Trina said she was on her way about five minutes ago."

"Speak of the devil," Cat says.

Trina's black Jeep pulls into the parking lot, leaving a space between her car and Cat's Camry. The sheen on the Jeep makes the car bright black, like the facets of obsidian, cool and aloof; the off-roader could make you roadkill and its pistons wouldn't skip a beat. It only complimented Trina's sharp looks even more.

Her hair is scrunchied up and sun-caressed; she wears shades that weren't picked up at a dollar store, but from a more thrifty scene. Her *GreenWaze* shirt is the same as Yolanda's, the black and green inverted. The vegan head of the market vendors has her arm wrapped around a potted plant. Based on her march alone, Trina does not look happy.

"She looks a little mad, but I like her fit," Yolanda says.

"Oh, I should match it, I gotta match her energy," Cat says as she digs through her bag, slipping on a different pair of shades with pineapples for frames.

"Am I vegan enough?"

"Shut up," Yolanda laughs, standing up to greet Trina.

"Hey, Tri," Yolanda says.

"Hi, Yola."

She sets the pot down on the table hard enough to sprinkle it with some soil.

"Can you believe no one else is showing up today? I have a hundred of these things to distribute around town, and the whole chat decided today was a great day to go ghost. Unbelievable, un-fucking-believable!"

Up close to what Trina brought with her, Cat ogles at the oddity.

It's some kind of pitcher plant. Craned like a question mark, it struggles to hold up its large, paunchy digestive tube that gives the plant its distinctive shape and name. Bold, shapeless stripes of incandescent blues, violets, reds and yellows run along the length of the pitcher's trap and sac. Frills flare like eyelashes, though, on closer inspection, some are more like spines.

This is the strangest plant she has ever seen in her life.

Cat tuned out Trina's rant, incurring some of her wrath.

"Are you even listening? Why are you even here?"

Cat snaps her eyes at her.

"To be a supportive friend," she says with a tinge of contempt.

"And you're eating the merchandise—"

"Trina," Yolanda cuts her off, "Take five, you're doing it again."

Deep breaths.

"I'm sorry, I just want to be good at my job and be a cute little vendorina and it's really difficult when you have to babysit other people. I'm taking a smoke break, I don't mean to target you, Cat. You're not on my team, and if you're not on my team, you're against me, but that's the kind of behavior and mindset my therapist has been talking me through and telling me that it's not a good bar to hold others to and that stable, healthy relationships shouldn't have a value assigned to them. It's a whole thing. I'm just regurgitating words right now. I'm deflecting, I... I'll be back."

Trina strides swiftly to the clearing on the other half of the lot. Cat and Yola are having trouble processing Trina's nervous breakdown, and the silence between them is immense.

After a few beats of quiet, Cat returns her attention to the plant Trina brought.

"So... what is this thing?"

"Oh, yeah, this is what it's all about," Yola sighs.

She swipes through her phone and pulls up a text from the groupchat with details relating to the plant.

"Since Greenwaze first made a Kickstarter, this plant has made its rounds online, and we were able to make our goal within a month, which was really surprising to us."

"Wow, congrats," Cat smiles.

"Thank you," Yolanda curtsies. "Trina is one of the heads of the campaign, so we've been doing a lot of running around the last two weeks and neither of us have been getting that much sleep, so yeah."

"Damn..." Cat whispers.

"Oh, and the guy who supplies these plants to us gave a list of names that it apparently goes by. Its monikers include but are not limited to 'the Lionfish Flower, Hummingbird's Paradise, the Caiman's Carafe, Aztec Amphora, Dust Devil's

Decanter…' I'm pretty sure this guy just made up all these names himself."

Cat pours them both more lemonade iced tea. "Probably did it to market it to a wider audience. Can you license and patent a plant, like is that allowed?"

"They did it with Chia Pets," Yola says between sips.

"That's true…"

"It's also called 'El Hambriento,' or 'O Faminto,'" Yolanda carefully pronounces the last two names.

"The Hungry One?" Catalina asks; her friend shrugs.

She continues to inspect the spines, their length radiating from the center where the mouth of the pitcher connects to the stalk and receptacle. Yola sits back in her beach chair, continuing to scroll through the texts.

"He says the origins of the plant are unknown, seeming to have a disparate range between Arizona to as far as the Atacama Desert in South America. It might have been found in isolated oasis—oasises…? Oases in either environment, though the necessary literature is lacking."

Yolanda pauses to sip her iced tea.

"It's suspected to be part of the pitcher plant family, but what genus it falls under is still up for debate until proper DNA sequencing can be done, as it was completely unknown up until a few years ago and is a rare variety at that. Until recent human efforts have allowed for its population to recover, it's critically endangered in the wild…"

"Does it say all that on the Kickstarter page, too?" Cat asks.

"Y'know, I don't remember. Shit, before I forget, I didn't even show you how it works."

"How it works? Does it do tricks?" Cat furrows her brow.

"Something like that."

Yolanda's little hands slip themselves into a pair of cream colored gardening gloves—at least they were cream at some point. They're stained with who knows how many years of dirt along the fingertips and the smooth patch for the palm. She reaches beneath her table and presents a plastic container and a plastic cup.

"Allow me to demonstrate. This is a Tupperware and this is a cup, right? Hold these.

She tosses them to Cat, who almost drops them onto the floor. A plate is set on the table by the curious plant.

Yolanda smirks, "Brace yourself, this has a tough smell."

With a delicate grip, Yolanda unfurls a leafy structure that acts as a lid to the bulbous jar-shaped head of the plant. The stench is immediate and vicious—a cross between lemon scented cleaning products and concentrated ammonia. Garden tweezers in her other hand, she reveals a half digested plastic food container lathered in some kind of goop and lays it on the plate. Catalina looks on in awe. She plucks out what is left of the plastic cup, only a small wrinkled sheet compared to what it was before.

Catalina is dumbstruck. "Does this thing eat plastic?"

"Not only does it eat plastic, it digests pretty much any man-made polymer based material, from rubber to vinyl; its interior is lined with acids so corrosive it only takes days for this thing to break down iron and steel. Guess how long it took for it to do this to the Tupperware?"

Cat shrugs.

"I put it in this morning," Yolanda chirps.

Cat's eyes grow wider. "H-how?"

"Strange, isn't it? The guy who sold these plants to us said that they don't yet know how it's able to digest plastic, but they suspect a correlation between other pitcher plants and the digestive enzymes they make to break down their prey. This plant seems to produce an even stronger set of enzymes that can eat almost any waste humans produce. This is a game changer, Cat. We're going to make waves with this thing."

The hulking sound of a four thousand pound 2018 Jet Black Jeep Wrangler barreling behind the two girls breaks the conversation. They jump on their feet, Trina pumps the brakes, swiftly parking parallel to the main tent. Trina's face isn't as flushed or anxious, and the smell of freshly toasted pot pervades the air.

"Oh, good, you're showcasing the plant," Trina says as she leaps down from the Jeep. "Do you want one?" she asks Cat.

"What? Oh, I mean—"

"We have a ton, and it would really mean a lot to us if you could help spread the word about it."

"This is what Greenwaze is all about," Yolanda says. "To spread awareness of this plant and to have it become a part of the way we dispose of waste. This could revolutionize every major industry; this can forever change the way we look at how we take care of the planet. We only need enough people supporting this movement."

"Dude, imagine this," Trina waves haphazard hands in front of Cat's face.

"Landfills, but instead, they're like... gardens... where these plants eat up whatever plastic doesn't get recycled. But we have to see its effectiveness over time, y'know, monitor its health and all that stuff. It seems to be a low maintenance plant, it's perfect. Buy one—no, take one. It's on the house."

Cat scratches her ear.

"I dunno, this kind of seems too good to be true."

She really doesn't want to entertain Trina any more than she has to.

"Please!" Trina composes herself, correcting her desperation. "Look, even though we reached our initial goal online, we're still a pretty small company. We need all the funding we can get to grow more of these on a larger scale and, before we can do that, we need to show everyone that this thing works. We're spearheading a revolution and you don't want to be a part of that? We're even giving you one for free."

"I'm not really the revolutionary type," Cat says.

She takes another glance at the Lionfish Flower, basking in the sun; a light breeze billows through the gazebo.

"So it just lives off of plastic, and that's it?"

"And sunlight and water like any other plant," Yolanda says. "Keep it well lit in some good soil, feed it some compost every now and then to get it started, and it'll do the rest."

Trina begins unloading more plants from her trunk, and hands Cat a large clay pot with a diameter wider than her torso. Cat peers into the pot with a sprinkle of disappointment, no suggestion or implication of the vibrant ferocity the little seedling will soon become.

"Couldn't I get a plant that's more… plant?"

Trina audibly winces. "Unfortunately, we don't have enough of them in full bloom that aren't already reserved, but it shouldn't take more than a couple months for it to get going."

Lightning strikes from afar. Cat parts ways with Yola and Trina, heading back to her car. Thunder follows. She buckles the pot in the passenger seat, and has her GPS set for home.

Cat hauls the pot from her car to her backyard, following Trina and Yolanda's instructions.

It shouldn't be so hard.

She has the house to herself. Her roommates are gone until Friday, with enough of the weekend to settle in before school starts back up on Monday. A thunderstorm shoulders its way through the sky, amassing a following and taking other clouds head on.

It rains for six hours. At least, on and off. Maybe. Cat wasn't paying attention. She sends one of her roommates, Marnie, a text asking how she's doing; no response.

Before then, she calls her friend Ále from back home, but she's at work right now.

Cat texts Diego.

Hey Diggy, you free to hang out later?

sorry homie im tryna taek a nap b4 wrk. Talk soon ✌

That can't be everyone, can it? At least, that's everyone she bothers keeping in touch with; Marnie, her other

roommate Synthia, Diggy, Alejandra, her mom. She just
hung out with Yola earlier, and Cat feels like she'd be
demanding too much of her friend's time if she asked to
hang out again. What's the cool down period for hanging out
with friends? Cat thinks about calling her mom, but she
knows she's busy, too.

🌲 🌲 🌲

Four in the afternoon is the loneliest hour on a rainy day
with nothing to do. She can't even smoke her cigarettes.
Like a Pavlovian response, simply looking at the empty pack
on her dresser simulates the taste of softly burnt tobacco in
her mouth. She groans, allowing the nicotine to taunt her a
little longer.

She opens Instagram, scrolls through some memes and
recent posts, closes the app and hops onto Twitter. She blinks
and it's already past seven. Her laptop plays a show she's
already binged several times this summer; she just wants to
fill the space with sound.

**Sorry my phone died earlier! I'm having dinner with the fam
right now, can we talk later?**

The rest of the week passes by in a similar fashion.

Friday comes, her roommates settling back into the
house after the lazy summer. Marnie had brought back a dog
from home, a tiny black Chihuahua named Hustler
Magazine. It even says that on his name tag. Hustler
definitely lives up to his name, kind of, by incessantly
barking for food until someone feeds him. The first month
he'd been marking his territory all over the house, but at
least he was no longer biting Catalina or Synthia.

Catalina shows them the plant, or the would-be plant
were it still not a pot of soil drowning in rainwater. They
gawk, they taunt and tease.

"How could this plant really do that?" they ask. "It's
scientifically improbable," they say.

Hustler Magazine marks his territory and asserts his
dominance over the Lionfish Flower's pot. They muse over
the implications of such a miraculous thing, and as the first

cool breeze of autumn approaches, they move on. To commit to her latest enterprise, Cat uses some of her financial aid money to buy a garden trowel, a nice pair of heavy duty gloves, a rake, and hedge clippers.

In late September, the tiniest bud of precious healthy green begins to peek out from the soil, as if to make sure that it's safe to come out.

A single frail hair of white shivers in the crisp December air.

February passes and the first leaves bud.

A tiny green heart for St. Patrick's Day.

March and April bring heavy rains to the long yearning grass and earth. Cat reaches out to Yolanda and Trina about their crowdfunding campaign, but GreenWaze seems to have closed its doors for good. Yola and Trina lost contact with them months ago after some legal issues cropped up, but the long list of Non-Disclosure Agreements—NDAs—behind the company obscure what may or may not have happened. The hundreds of plants they had before are either dead or have already been sold.

 As Yolanda instructed, Catalina refills the pot with soil at least once a month, making sure that all her old banana and orange peels and apple cores and leftover food that went bad after sitting in her fridge for a week made its way into the compost bin, and from there, onto the lap of the Lionfish Flower. Aided by the reinvigorated heat and humidity, and drenched in more water than it's ever had, the plant finally, properly, grows a stalk in May, in time for everyone to leave again.

Catalina and her roommates renew their lease to the house a second time, and they drive back south and east, while Cat once again has the whole place to herself for three months of solitude. The plant thrives.

Saturday nights in this college town are not that eventful right now. Most of the fun people either fled south for the summer or are making their own mischief at home or with friends.

Catalina used to like her personal space, but having a three-bed, two-bath house to pace around in gets old after the first month. She has a bike she neglects until she guilts herself into riding it. She smokes cigarettes in her backyard, her front yard, in her car, on her open windowsill, watering her plants, feeding the Lionfish Flower, walking around the abandoned school campus, at the park when no one's around to judge her, before catching a movie at the theater, after the movie ends, walking around the neighborhood, on her bike that she often neglects, but only the one time—smoking and exercising don't really go well together.

She spends a lot of time outside. It gives her something to do, eases some of that anxiety, pack after pack. The stink of tobacco clings to her fingers as she sits on her deck overlooking the backyard. Her rake lays on the ground, gazing up at nothing. Since she has nowhere to store it, she sets it upright against the deck. The deck itself is not very tall or big, just a foot or two above the ground and enough to tightly pack a group of ten, maybe. The light above the door is that harsh orange-yellow that's not energy efficient. *If only these trees could talk.*

Trees apparently use mycelium to communicate amongst themselves. They send each other chemical responses and even nutrients through this grand living underground network, like how people use the internet, carrying whole conversations and keeping each other in the know about news in the forest, or something like that. She learned about it from a YouTube video. The secrets plants and trees know that humans do not is a subject that continues to root itself deeper into Catalina's mind, branching into other aimless thoughts.

What wonders never cease in the life of a world-weary oak? How do plants know to attract bees and hummingbirds and other animals? How do plants know what time it is? Why does the willow weep—for love lost or unrequited? To mourn family or friends? Maybe they're disconnected, left out, or self-secluded. They tend to be found hunching over rivers and lakes, looking for something they lost, something that's more precious than what the rest of the world can offer. Maybe they're depressed and there's nothing more to it.

"People aren't just depressed for no reason, Cat," she tells herself.

She takes a long drag from her cigarette, the cloud of smoke swirling in her lungs. She tries to visualize it. Her stomach groans, and she checks the time on her phone: 3:49 a.m. She puts out the cigarette, flicks it into the ashtray beside her, and stretches. Making her way onto her feet, a shadow flickers out of view.

She freezes.

It was probably a bird. Maybe even a bat.

She goes to head into the house and a pot breaks behind her.

She turns the flash on for her phone and walks down the stairs of the deck to inspect.

Her succulents are gone, some cacti are missing; clay pots shattered, soil dashed across the ground. She's chased off raccoons and possums before, but she's never known them to go for her succulents or cacti. Marnie was unsuccessfully growing some tomatoes before and even their pots were dashed across the ground. She's not going to be happy about that, either.

Great. Fuck me for taking up a hobby, right?

She walks backward towards the stairs, scanning the backyard with her phone. Something blurs right past her and hits her shoulder.

She yelps from the sudden attack from behind. She chucks it aside, sending her rake twirling a few feet away. It was only the rake.

I should invest in an outdoor shed or something.

Another loud crash, from the front yard—the garbage bins sound like they're being knocked over again.

Of course, it has to be raccoons or something, they've been at it for months now, going through the trash late at night, making a huge mess, knocking over the damn bins.

Her Lionfish Flower has been doing a pretty decent job with the garbage she gives it, but its mouth and pouch are still too tiny to take on most of her trash. Plus, there's only so much that the flower can process at a time.

And, of course, her bins are tipped over.

"God dammit."

She decides to leave it for tomorrow. Looping back around to the deck, her lionfish plant stands like a tiny guard, barely a foot tall. She pauses, staring at the flower. She may have been too panicky before, though she does find it odd that it's the only plant left unscathed.

"Keep an eye out, will ya?" she tells the plant, entering her house to call it a night.

🌲 🌲 🌲

When Marnie and Synthia return at the end of summer break, they share some pizza and wine the night they show up and reflect on all the memories they've made in this house. It had been so long that the two completely forgot about the Lionfish Flower. Cat leads them to the early evening air, her footsteps excited and giddy. The sun lays on its belly, hidden behind the houses and trees off to the west. Hustler Magazine makes a dash for the pots and plants to piss on.

"Come on, guys, we're losing daylight out here!" she calls out to them.

"We're coming, it's not like it's going anywhere," Marnie muses.

"Fair warning, this thing smells absolutely terrible," Cat says.

"Holy..."

"Yo…"

The stench immediately slams their nostrils with the unmistakable fragrance of molten plastic, boiled battery acid, the unholy waft of a garbage truck making its way across the neighborhood, and friction. Marnie and Synthia gag; Cat has acclimated to the smell by now.

It's bloomed even bigger than Cat could have ever hoped. The flower stands at an impressive five feet tall, its tallest spikes reaching near Cat's own five foot five. Dozens of spines flared like a porcupine mated with a round bristle brush. Black marks, like a thousand Rorschach paintings, blot along the length of the pitcher's gullet; super saturated reds and yellows clash against electric blue rivulets. The pattern reminds Catalina of poisonous frogs native to the Amazon. In short, don't look at this plant while you're stoned.

Synthia cleans her glasses with her shirt. "Cat, what have you been feeding this thing?" she asks.

"Everything," Cat replies with a self-congratulatory smile.

"And it really works? Does it actually eat plastic?" Marnie asks.

"Oh, so much more than that. Why don't you try it out yourself, throw something in."

"How about I do something small? I don't want it to blow up or something," Marnie says.

"Don't worry, it can handle just about anything," Cat says. "The smell says it all."

Marnie dips back into the house to offer the Lionfish Flower a pair of beaten up boots from her closet. As soon as she returns to the backyard, she gags again, scrunching up her face in disgust.

Cat remembers how Marnie wore those boots all throughout their freshman and sophomore years together. The faded black leather is warped around the ankles and the toe box, riddled with creases from years of walking and running. The insole of the left boot, ripped open on a hiking trip to some canyons in Georgia in the spring, has gradually widened along the length of the foot that half of the sole is able to flap like a Muppet's mouth.

"These boots have served me well. It's time they get a proper retirement," Marnie says.

She gently drops the boots down the swollen throat of the Devil's Decanter. Synthia picks up Hustler Magazine.

"Stop it, you wouldn't!" Marnie shrieks, snatching her Chihuahua from a cackling Synthia.

"I'm kidding, I'm kidding!" she insists.

Covering her mouth to block the smell, Synthia tosses a pizza box into the plants mouth, amazed that the mouth is big enough to house it.

Both girls are in utter disbelief.

"Cat, this thing is like a living trash compactor!" Synthia shouts.

"I know, it's unbelievable," Cat says.

Marnie wipes her hair and sweat off her brow, "It really took a full year for this thing to grow?"

"Pretty much. It's kind of beautiful... Would be perfect without the smell, though."

Marnie releases a wet belch that definitely had some acid reflux. "I don't wanna be rude because this is a pretty and magical flower and you worked so hard on it, but can we go back inside? This thing reeks."

Two days later, there's a single strip of leather and barely anything left of Marnie's shoelaces from her boots. This convinces Cat's roommates to start throwing away their stuff into the Lionfish Flower, too.

Yola arrived in town the night after Marnie and Synthia did, so Catalina sharing her side project with her in person for the first time in months was well worth the wait. She had been sending videos and TikToks of herself throwing random garbage into the lionfish, and she's found that entertaining enough. Like Yola and Trina had said way back when, it really does eat just about anything, lightbulbs, old rugs, entire trash bags full of garbage, heavy duty cardboard boxes, even rusty bicycles.

By Yolanda's request, when the Caiman's Carafe got big enough to start breaking down their unwanted junk, Cat began logging down what it can eat and how long it takes to digest each load, and she realizes, over time that, the bigger it grows and the more of a particular material it digests, the faster it can break it down.

Nothing says spring cleaning like doing it in summer. Even while purging through all her old stuff, she still leaves more of a mess than when she started.

🌲 🌲 🌲

Several Thursdays pass, and on one such Thursday in early October, Cat is doing homework in her bedroom, windows open to air out her smoking, some light indie music playing in the background. Night begins to creep in. Hustler Magazine keeps racing in and out of her room and through the rest of the house. Taking a little break from her studies, Catalina sets some ramen noodles to boil and collects the trash around the kitchen to toss into the Lionfish Flower. She enters the backyard, bag in hand, and Hustler Magazine scurries close behind her. She leaves the door open so he can run back inside. He does his business in the grass, and Cat sets down the bag next to some others queued up for disposal. It's so far one of the only downsides until the plant gets bigger, if it even can; it can only take on a trash bag or two at a time, and these are the heavy duty ones for tall kitchen cans.

The Lionfish Flower stands at the center of the garden, at least what's left of it. It's now the only plant that's outlived all the others Cat started to grow, which makes maintaining this one a lot easier. She opens the lid to the flower's trap, and tosses a bag in. She notices that its leaves are looking a little faint and spotty.

That's new.

The days are getting shorter, and the weather's starting to chill again; the flower hasn't experienced its first proper winter yet, and she has no idea how it'll fare, not even Yola, whose own Lionfish Flowers have had mixed success surviving the cold season.

She texts Yola to ask her what remedies she can try to help out her plant. Her ramen is boiling over. It starts bubbling and leaking water onto the stovetop, Cat hurries inside to turn the stove off and remove the pot from the heat. Paper towels? No, she goes for a cloth towel, and it still burns her because the water was boiling.

Of course, she thinks, but it's not too bad.

Deciding to wait until the water itself is cooler to clean up, she serves herself and slurps some very soft noodles.

The dog starts barking.

"Hustler, get back in the house," she calls out.

He starts yelping—he's never yelped like that before.

She dashes out the back, and the poor thing is screaming. Cat scans the grass around her, not sure where he is.

"Hustler? Hustler? Where are you?"

As she was finishing that sentence, she looks directly forward.

The dog is inside the plant.

She panics, "Oh shit! How did you get in there?"

Cat scrambles for the gardening gloves off the table by the deck, and sticks her left hand, not her dominant hand, down the gullet of the lionfish's sac and yanks Hustler out.

The poor dog is okay, but patches of his fur and skin are singed by the corrosive bile the plant produces. She whisks him to the bathtub inside to clean him off as best as she can.

The front door swings open, she can hear her roommates shuffling in and carrying their conversation from outside.

"Hey, Cat, you here?" Synthia asks.

"In the bathroom," she calls out. They make their way over, and Marnie shrieks at the sight of her dog. Hustler is riddled with dozens of burn marks.

"What the hell happened, Cat?!"

"I don't know—"

"What do you mean? How did this happen?" She bundles her dog in a towel.

"I mean, I don't know. He must have jumped into the flower somehow. I was making ramen so I didn't see it happen, I'm so sorry, Marnie."

Marnie coddles her traumatized Chihuahua, who hasn't blinked much since Cat rescued him.

"I find that very unlikely."

"What, me making ramen?"

"That he got in there by himself."

"He had to. I was cooking... Marnie, you're not seriously accusing me of doing this on purpose, are you?"

Marnie breaks eye contact. "All I know is that you were watching my dog while I was gone, and he ended up getting half-digested by your freaky ass plant. He was under your watch. He somehow made it in there."

"I'm sorry, I have no idea how he got in there, it happened so fast, but I can assure you, I did not do this to your dog."

"No, you did this to me," Marnie storms out of the tiny bathroom.

"What the hell are you talking about? Marnie? Marnie!"

"House meeting!" Marnie shouts from the living room. The last time they held one was when they had to reaffirm that the bathrooms and kitchens should be clean for the next person to use.

"I know that we all lead busy lives, but this is completely unacceptable. This is my dog. Hustler is family. I put trust in you guys and he trusts the both of you—"

"Hold up, I didn't feed your dog to the plant," Synthia says.

"I didn't feed your dog to the plant, either!" Cat adds.

"You've been acting super weird since we got it."

"Enough!" Marnie turns to Cat, "Look, I recognize that your goal is an ambitious one, but it's not worth it if it's going to start eating people."

"It's not eating people," Cat says.

"It tried to eat Hustler! Hustler is people, too, Catalina."

They hear the bins from the front yard topple and crash onto the pavement.

"Oh, what the hell! Those damn trash pandas are at it again," Cat shouts.

"Forget them, we're having a house meeting right now, that can wait."

"I'm checking on them—"

"For what, to see if you have any more garbage to sort through so you can tend to your freaky flower? Or are you going to feed them to your plant, too? You're sick, Cat. You smell like rotten food all the time and you can't even carry a conversation anymore without bringing the damn thing up. We're getting rid of it."

The three of them peek through the blinders of their living room window, and see raccoons hopping out of the bins.

"At least they're leaving," Synthia says.

While Marnie pouts on the couch, Cat and Synthia go to the front yard, and before they can straighten up the bins again, they both see a raccoon tail, but not the raccoon it belongs to.

A strange crunching and hissing noise comes from around the corner of the house.

In the gentle shadows of the early evening, a large crooked figure hunches low, and it lunges for Cat and Synthia, a short lunge at that. Its movement is sluggish, awkward, lacking balance and grace, like a toddler trying to walk by themself. Cat and Synthia are in shock to see the Lionfish Flower craned before them, raising its bulbous heavy head. It stands on knobbly, knuckled roots. A group of tendrils picks up a raccoon from the ground, where it lied still, and sinks the poor creature into its mouth. Hissing, bubbling sounds emanate from the head of the Hummingbird's Paradise, though it's more like the Hummingbird's Hell. It's digesting the raccoon whole.

Cat and Synthia trample over each other in their race back inside the house; they lock the door, slide the latch and bolt it shut. Marnie asks what happened and, though they do their best to tell her, she doesn't believe them.

"I swear, it literally ate a raccoon right in front of us!" Synthia shouts.

"But… it's impossible, plants don't walk around, guys, that's literally what makes them plants," Marnie says.

Cat calls Yolanda, but it keeps going to voicemail.

"You don't think we know that? Doesn't make any sense to me either, and weren't you the one saying it was trying to eat people? It's straight up eating animals now," Cat says, waving her hands at the window. "If you don't believe us, look outside."

"No, thank you," Marnie's face loses some color, "I've seen what it did to my dog."

"What the hell do we do?" Synthia asks.

"I'm trying to figure that out, Yola's not picking up any of my calls."

"Maybe her plant tried to eat her, too," Marnie says. "Oh, god, what did you do, Cat?"

The call goes to voicemail again. Cat crouches behind the blinds and peeks through them; she watches the Lionfish Flower haphazardly flop along the grass. She attempts to sound as composed as possible.

"Hey Yola, it's Cat, uh… a little update: the plant you gave me a while ago is trying to eat me and my roommates, it's running around in my front yard. What the fuck do we do to get rid of it? Did you know it could do this? Please call me back, I need to know if you're okay."

Cat paces around the tile floor in deep erratic thought, checking her phone to see if Yola replied. The other two girls crouch behind the window blinds, watching the lionfish plant sitting on a browning patch of grass. They can't see what it's looking at, or if it can even see at all. Marnie soothes her dog and applies some ointment to his burns.

"It's just a plant," Marnie says, "Can't we just kill it like one?"

"I don't know," Synthia says, "It'd make sense, but I'm not sure how we can practically kill something like that."

"We have to try. It traumatized my baby for life," she says, gently petting the Chihuahua's head. "Cat?"

Cat pauses her anxious pacing, "Here me out, guys."

"No, no, we're not keeping this thing!" Marnie shouts.

"Are you serious? Dude!" Synthia adds.

"This plant is a miracle plant, it can eat trash, it's like a goat mixed with a garbage disposal, but way better."

"Do you hear yourself?" Synthia stands at eye level with Cat. "This thing literally devoured an animal twice the size of Hustler in a matter of seconds and could easily kill one of us. Why do you still want to keep it after that?"

"Has Yola gotten back to you?" Marnie asks.

Cat checks her phone again, the long text she sent to her remains unread.

What the hell?

"This plant was supposed to change the world," Cat says, "I saw it happen before my eyes."

She reflects on the scant research that was done on the plant when she first heard about it last summer.

Maybe that's what happens when something that isn't well understood is used for financial gain.

Cat runs her hands through her hair in an attempt to soothe herself.

She faces both her roommates with a sigh, "Look, if it ate the raccoon, and all the other trash it had today, it still has to process all of that. It'll do it quick, but if we want to get rid of it, we have to give it something way too big for it to eat. We do that, we can probably kill it."

The three of them don layers of thick sweatshirts and jackets for padding and protection, scarves, hats, gloves and boots. They look like they're about to walk through a snowstorm, not march into battle with an oversized carnivorous plant.

What's the appropriate thing to wear for that anyway? Cat thinks.

She grabs her phone, her cigarettes and lighter and stuffs them into the pocket of her jacket. Even though they're a month deep into autumn, the weather is a tad humid for the blizzard-ready look, and they gather the gardening tools from the backyard. Synthia takes the shovel, Marnie the rake, and since they don't have bigger tools than that, Cat arms herself with the hedge clippers.

"Man, a chainsaw would be real handy right now," Synthia says.

Cat turns to her, "Chainsaws are not good for the environment because they run on gasoline—"

"Do you ever stop?" Marnie interrupts.

"Blame it on the plant," Cat shrugs.

They sneak their way into the front yard, crouching behind some bushes and the A/C unit. They get a clear view of the lawn, but no sign of the plant nearby. It's not hiding behind the cars either.

"Guys… where did it go?"

"Let's check down the street, it can't be that far," Cat says.

"This is getting out of control," Synthia adds, "Should we call the police?"

"What the hell do we tell them, that a pitcher plant woke up and chose violence and is at large in our neighborhood? I doubt they'd buy that," Marnie says.

"Yola still isn't returning any of my calls. It looks like we're on our own with this one."

The rest of the neighborhood sinks behind the silhouettes of loblolly pines and bald cypress trees looming over the horizon. The only light comes from neighboring houses and the streetlamps; their glow drenches everything in an unnaturally saturated orange. The girls go from lawn to lawn, checking under cars and following the stormpath the plant left behind, the knocked down garbage bins, half eaten dogs and stray cats screeching in pain, the sight enough to make the girls retch. Mailbox poles end abruptly, standing as witnesses to the gluttony of it all.

Several houses down the bend, a big party blasts the eclectic hi-hats and undulating 808s of trap, the whole spectrum of light flashing like a club. A pair of college guys in swim trunks and flip flops sit atop the hood of a car, parked by a dozen or so others scattered across the lawn.

"Hey, ladies," the brunette rocking puka shells yells. He slurs his words through his clear plastic cup, "This is a certified rager we're having here, been running for twenty-four hours straight! Why don't y'all come over and hang?"

"If it's such a rager, why aren't you inside?" Synthia asks.

"Ignore him," his friend says, parting back his long dreads, "We're just getting some fresh air."

"Y'all are pretty overdressed for the surf party," the drunk one says.

"Hey, random question," Marnie steps forward, "Have you seen a giant man-eating pitcher plant around here?"

"Is that code for something?" one boy asks the other.

"Over there!" Synthia shouts, pointing behind the cars. The Lionfish Flower is digging through the copious amounts of trash full of empty beer cans and used cups. The girls duck behind a blue Jetta.

"Ok, you see the trash can?" Cat gestures to the large green bin behind the monster. "We gotta make sure it goes inside it so we can take it back to our place. So, we flank him, toss him in and get out. Be as discreet as possible."

"I don't think discretion is a problem for us," Synthia says, glancing back at the drunk party people stumbling in and out of the house.

"Still. I'll grab the trash," Cat says, "You guys make sure it goes in. You ready?"

Her roommates nod. They split up and weave through the parked cars, only a few feet away from the Aztec Amphora. It jerks its head, the heavy bass thumping from the house. Marnie and Synthia are behind a car parked in front of the pile of garbage bags and heap of beer boxes.

The two girls empty out the trash bin. Cat grabs a bag of garbage and hurls it, spooking the Lionfish Flower. Its long tendrils and leaf stems fan out and grapple her. Cuts from her hedge clippers leave stubs and frayed ends, but the creature keeps tangling her in more of its wiry vine-like arms. The painful hiss it makes is acidic and gurgly, akin to hot oil on a frying pan. It lifts her mere inches from the ground. Her layers of clothes, the winter gloves, and being bound and throttled by vines render Cat in an awkward position to cut through the plant material.

Synthia leaps forth and slaps the flat of her shovel across the pitcher plant's head; Marnie scrapes and slashes the tendrils, tangling some up in her prongs. Cat manages to snip herself free, clutches for a trash bag at her feet, and runs into the plant, the bag as a cushion, bashing the Caiman's Carafe with her whole weight. It topples into the open trash bin, and Synthia shuts the lid; light and nimble Marnie hops on top to keep the lid closed. Cat snags a half drunk bottle of Vodka carelessly thrown away, and she and Synthia drag the bin with them across the lawn and onto the street. The monster bangs against the inside of the container, slamming itself around.

"Hey, that's not your trash!" The drunk guy from before yells at them.

"Shut up, Puka Shells," Synthia shouts.

"Yeah, shut up, Puka Shells!" Marnie taunts.

"Can't tell girls nothing anymore without getting shat on, even when they're literally leaving you for trash," he tells his friend who is babysitting him.

"Man, shut the hell up, Puka Shells," his friend says.

The girls haul the bin back to their yard as Marnie rides the garbage bin.

"What do we do now?" Marnie asks.

"Now," Cat says, lighter and vodka bottle in hand, "We light this bitch on fire."

She stuffs her scarf inside, sparks fly, and she's ready to throw it. Marnie jumps off the bin, the carnivorous Carafe bursts from the trash. Its ferocious spines flare, more tendrils shake violently, and its giant mouth sac stretches wide, catching Catalina whole. The oddly dynamic motion flows the way a pelican would scooping a fish from out the water.

Synthia and Marnie screech in horror.

They slap and slam and scratch and rake the monster with their garden tools, but it's not as effective as before. If the Devil's Decanter could roar like a bear or a lion, it definitely would now. Instead, it merely gurgles and fizzles like a balloon.

The lionfish topples down with the bin, flopping over with a thud onto the hard asphalt that meets the pavement of the driveway. Marnie and Synthia see something stretch the outer skin of the plant's engorged gullet—Cat's hedge trimmers pierce through, acid sprays out and singes their clothes. Cat is drenched in a blinding light, her vision blotched with the after image seared into her retinas.

Catalina's little hands tear with great struggle the open wound she made, and she crawls out from the goo and undigested waste of the beast. She coughs, spitting excessively to get the taste of battery acid and sulphur and frat party garbage out of her mouth; the smell is worse than anything dead or alive she's ever had the displeasure to whiff. For the few moments she was in the lionfish's stomach, it devoured some of her hair and left burns on her face and neck, the rest of her body protected by the many layers of clothes.

Her roommates flock to Cat; somebody parked on the road in front of their driveway. Two people emerge from the car, the high beams blaring at the trio. Yola crouches to help Cat sit up, Trina standing behind her. Both their faces are draped with horror and disgust at the sight of the mighty pitcher plant slayer.

"Are you okay?" Yola asks.

Cat groans to affirm she's alright.

Synthia, Marnie and Yola help their friend back to her feet. Yola kicks the plant back into the trash bin; Cat stops her, igniting the molotov cocktail she took with her into the plant's stomach. She sets the whole thing ablaze in the middle of the street. Burnt plastic fills the midnight air, the toxic fumes drive all the girls back inside.

Marnie applies some ointment from her first aid kit onto Cat's face and neck, it looks topical for the most part. Her forehead and cheeks look especially burnt, as if she were branded by a Carnevale mask still hot with iron. Marnie and Synthia sit with Cat on the couch, Yola takes a seat behind the coffee table to face them. Trina leans on the wall by the door.

"What the hell, Yola?" Cat pauses, "I thought you were dead!"

"I lost my phone while dealing with my own Lionfish Flowers. I'm glad everyone's okay, too."

"Did you two know?" Marnie asks.

Yola and Trina glance at each other, Yola gets fidgety and breaks eye contact.

"Not—"

Trina's eyes pierce at Yola.

"... the whole time." Yola's voice is low.

"You've got to be kidding me," Synthia says.

"So you knew they could just eat us?" Cat straightens up in her seat on the couch, "You knew that they could just go on a stroll and start a feeding frenzy at any time?"

"We had no idea until yesterday that they could walk," Yola said.

"That's a likely story," Marnie scoffs.

"Walking is definitely not the only thing it can do," Synthia says.

"It's a plant that can digest metal, of course they knew," Catalina says.

"I've had my suspicions," she adds, "The ones I had were at it for months, but I didn't have any proof until I caught them on camera. I couldn't say anything because I signed an NDA. We both did."

"Jesus Christ," Synthia says.

"Can't you contact the company you two worked for?" Cat asks. "They have to pay for this shit, we're probably not the only ones that went through this."

"There's so much red tape around Greenwaze, a metric crap ton of nothing but dense legal jargon and vague wishy washy answers—"

Cat's chest swells, "You're not their little lab rat anymore, Yola, why are you defending them?"

Yolanda shivers, and Cat, shaking in her seat, attempts to cool her tone.

"The company shutting down," Yola replies, "and going bankrupt exacerbated some of those issues, but it straight up disappeared. We have no way to contact them even if we wanted to and I have no idea what's going on with the higher ups. They ghosted me a long time ago."

"Greenwaze shut down its auxiliary operations, but it's not defunct or bankrupt, at least not yet," Trina breaks her silence. "Like Miss Pocketful of Sunshine said, there's a whole slew of NDAs floating around in limbo, stuff we can't even tell you, because if we do, it's a breach of contract and we'll be eyes deep in lawsuits. Plus, they're based somewhere in Central America, so we'd have to bring international law into play, and that gets expensive. American law has no authority wherever they are. All we know for sure is they're international."

"Which is how they were able to transport the plant to begin with," Marnie says. "They must have had it under some other merchandising category during shipment, using different procedure codes to their advantage."

"I cannot confirm nor deny because I have no idea how they did it," Trina says, stretching her arms out.

"I doubt 'carnivorous plant' has a merchandising category to fall under. There has to be some sort of international standard for stuff like this," Synthia says.

"Normal pitcher plants and venus fly traps probably would fall under that," Marnie adds, "They're just not going to eat people like this one does so it's not a major concern."

"You could buy a thousand crickets for twenty bucks on Amazon," Trina says, "Completely depreciate your local ecosystem for the amount it takes to fill up half a tank of gas. There's a lot of crazy shit money can buy."

"Ok, so what? That's it? A plant tries to kill us and there's nothing we can do?" Cat asks.

"Nothing," Trina says, "Unless…" She stealthily slides along the wall toward Cat; she's a bit facetious about it, too. Uncomfortably so.

"Should you want to take a case like this as high up as you can go, I can't legally recommend that you should contact the Feds and tell them all about this flower. That would be a breach of contract since this is a private company providing a specialized purpose with whom I can't disclose any internal information about. But you've already come upon this knowledge on your own, you're a firsthand source. Quick question for the class: what is the kind of procedural device that allows more than one plaintiff to charge a company in court?"

"Class action lawsuit," Marnie says, raising her hand.

Trina shrugs, "I cannot say nor imply that this would be a good alternative, I'm not a legal consultant. If you just so happen to, it would be on your own volition absent any outside coercion on my or Yolanda's part for you to pursue litigation for physical, mental and emotional damages due to a product that would surely be considered a life threatening hazard to the public if they knew about it."

Cat feels like a bag of sand is sitting on her head. "Wouldn't you also be roped into that because of your NDA? You were the ones that sold it to me."

"Do you have proof I knew?" Trina crosses her arms.

"Maybe you've been tipped with recently acquired footage from an anonymous source that wouldn't criminalize us with prior knowledge before selling the plant to you." Yola chimes in. "Plus, you already have your own evidence from over the summer."

Cat checks her phone. Sure enough, an unknown number has sent her a video attachment of the lionfish plants in Yolanda's backyard.

"Wow, you two are way too good at playing the whole morally ambivalent card," Marnie says.

"Running a business does that to you," Trina smirks with a wink.

"This is by far the most traumatic and bizarre night I've had in a long time," Cat says.

"Stranger things have happened though," Trina says. "Water bears are able to survive the vacuum of space, cockroaches are said to survive nuclear bombs, gingko trees withstood and prevailed after Hiroshima. Schrodinger's cat lives and dies in a box, and all our stories are written in our bones and on the wrinkles of our skin. The rainforests and the deserts of the world still hold many mysteries and secrets, both known and unknown, many creatures, endangered and not, but is it worth the venture if it means losing them at the same time? Is it worth knowing the unknowable if we lose ourselves in the process?"

Cat rolls her eyes, "Again, you were the one that sold this fucking thing to me!"

"And I will say it again, unless you have proof that states otherwise, you're hitting me with slander and I'll see your ass in court," Trina snorts. She spreads her hands on the coffee table, leveling her eyes to match Cat's gaze.

"You have a choice, Catalina, the cards are on the table. You have been wronged, all of us have, what the hell are you going to do about it?"

Beyond The Truth

Lies Reality

By

Mayura

Amarkant

"**A**ahh… Ravi! Aahh! Oh no! Help! Help me!"

Ravi was on the phone when a scream pierced through the air. It was Suruchi, his wife. He rushed to the bedroom expecting the worst. On his way, he tripped over the sofa and landed face down.

The screams were getting louder.

He scrambled towards her while shouting, "Coming, Suru! Coming!"

He entered the bedroom and his jaw dropped in shock.

She was lying there, half naked, holding a small teddy bear and staring at the wall where a cockroach was perched and defiantly staring back. Ravi watched her helplessly; she looked nothing like the attractive and elegant, dusky girl he married eighteen years ago. She appeared older than thirty-seven, with furrows on her forehead, disheveled hair, dry skin, parched lips and eyes that were shrouded in dark circles. Her body was bloated because of the drugs the psychiatrist had prescribed.

She saw him and lurched forward. It was quite a sight considering that she was hardly dressed and the room was in a mess.

"Help me, Ravi! Monster! Ravi, it's a monster, look! It's going to kill me, Ravi! Before it kills me, you kill it… or better still, kill me… just make it stop… make it stop, Ravi… please! Please!"

He stepped ahead and gathered her in his arms. She started howling loudly as he caressed her rough, knotted hair.

"It's okay, Suru, it's okay… I am here now… I will take care of everything."

After a while, the sobbing stopped and she fell asleep in his tired arms. She started snoring and snuggled into his hairy chest. He slept beside her for some time. About an hour later, he placed her on the bed and went to the living room. It was a windy June evening and the sky was threatening a downpour at any time.

A storm was also brewing inside Ravi and he didn't know how to calm it.

His train of thought was disturbed by the loud ring of the phone. He hurriedly answered it, lest Suruchi would wake up again. She got disturbed by the slightest noise and he wanted her to be asleep right now. There was so much to do, so much to think about, so many decisions to make.

After a couple of rings, the phone got disconnected and then rang again. He answered immediately. It was his mother.

"Is everything okay?" she asked in a worried tone.

"Yes, *Aai*…" his voice trailed off.

"Don't lie. It's her, isn't it?" she asked desperately.

"She has a name, *Aai*. Suruchi. And she is fine," he responded gruffly.

She replied firmly, "This is it! You need to send her to her mother's house. Your father and I insist! Enough is enough! If not for your own sanity, you must at least think about your kids—"

She kept blaring into the phone. He sighed and hung up mid-way. The phone rang again.

He yelled into the phone, "Yes! I got it! I got it! Stop calling me!"

"Hey, Ravi, it's me, Samir! Is everything okay?"

Ravi calmed himself and replied, "Oh, I am so sorry, Samir, I thought it was someone else. Tell me."

Samir chuckled and after a brief pause, he said, "I called you with good news and bad. What would you like to hear first?"

"All news is the same for me now. Tell me whatever you wish," replied Ravi listlessly as he shuffled his feet.

Samir cleared his throat and said, "Well, the good news is all the money has been transferred to your account. You got a good deal for the farmhouse in Karjat, despite these crazy times. The bad news is… you have nothing more to sell. You need to give the Jeep to the guy you sold it to by next Monday. You are officially bankrupt after you spend this last bit of money."

Ravi's heart sank as the words fell on his ears. He gathered himself, closed his eyes and clenched his fist.

He managed to whisper hoarsely, "What are my options?"

Samir paused before speaking and said softly, "The second wave has been a cruel blow, Ravi. The pandemic has left everyone in a lurch. Many people have-"

Ravi cut him mid-way.

"What are my options, Samir? You are my financial advisor later and friend first. C'mon, tell me," Ravi's voice trembled as tears welled up in his eyes.

Samir sighed and spoke in a matter-of-fact manner, "Alright then, here is the truth: your salons, restaurants and gyms have all closed down and we still need to pay everyone what we owe them. Your cars and office are already sold. Your home is on a mortgage, all your investments and *vaini*'s gold have been used up. Your farmhouse in Karjat was the last piece of property remaining, and, with it being sold, you are officially bankrupt. Your options are…"

Every word that Samir spoke after that made Ravi go numb. He gulped hard and sat down. His hands shook as he hung up on Samir.

The house was filled with Suruchi's snores and the fan was squeaking in rhythm. He fished out a handkerchief from his pocket and stuffed it in his mouth. He screamed, but no one could hear his muffled sounds. Tears were falling fast, but no one could see him crying. The walls were closing in on him as he curled up into the fetal position and kept sobbing quietly.

🌲 🌲 🌲

"*Saheb*! Oh, *Saheb*! Please wake up. It's time for *Madam*'s bath!"

It was Beena, their faithful housekeeper who came in at dawn and left after dinner every day.

Ravi rubbed his eyes as he slowly got up from the floor.

"What were you doing on the floor? Why didn't you have dinner last night? Was *Madam* okay last night? Is everything okay? What should I make for breakfast? Is *egg bhurji* fine?"

She started dusting the sofas while the questions tumbled out of her paan-stained mouth. Ravi glanced towards the bedroom, it was slightly ajar and everything inside was quiet.

Beena picked up the broom and started sweeping the house. As she bent, her bosom threatened to tumble out of her low-cut blouse. She wore a traditional nine-yard *sari* that allowed her to squat on the floor while sweeping or mopping. Despite the lockdown, she ensured that she reported to work every day, mostly because she wanted to get away from her drunk husband and partly so she could take care of her beloved *Madam, Saheb,* and kids.

Her curvy body brushed against the cluttered furniture as she swiftly maneuvered her way. She always ended up transferring the dust on the furniture much to her irritation since it increased her dusting chores. The chair screeched as she pushed it away to make way for her weapon of mass destruction, her broom. She suddenly realized she was causing a ruckus.

"Shh…*Madam* is still sleeping. Go wake the children," she sheepishly shushed herself and blabbered in a subdued voice.

Ravi watched Beena leave the room as he yawned and stretched his muscular arms and looked out of the window. Birds were twittering as the morning sun rose, and the sun made designs on the walls as it streamed through the leaves. The cooing of a cuckoo came from a distance. He soaked in the morning peace and felt a quiet sense of relief as he made his way to the bathroom.

Suruchi hardly slept through the night. Today was a rare morning. A gut feeling told him that it was going to be a great day. Suruchi was going to be in a good mood and that meant the whole home would resonate with laughter. He smiled to himself and started brushing his teeth.

A blood curdling scream rang through the house. It was Beena. He dropped the toothbrush and ran; the wails coming from Suruchi's room.

Beena was standing over the bed sobbing uncontrollably. He took one look at Suruchi and slumped on to the floor.

Ravi's seven-year-old daughter, Rinky, came running into the room, wondering what the commotion was about. She froze at the door and clung to her father, frightened because of Beena's loud cries.

His sixteen-year-old-son, Omkar, entered the scene and shouted loudly.

"We have to call a doctor… *Baba*, call Dr. Murthy now!"

Ravi appeared to be in a deep state of shock and wasn't moving. He just kept staring at the bed. Suruchi was lying there, clutching the teddy bear's legs with both hands, the rest of the toy inside her mouth. Dried blood was at her nostrils, her hair was ruffled, and there were scratch marks on her entire body. She lay there naked; half covered by the blanket. Her eyes were blood red and popping out, her cheeks stained with dried tears. It was an unimaginable scene.

Omkar's body was quivering in fear. When he realized that he had to play adult, he nervously dialed the doctor and the police in quick succession.

Twenty minutes later, the police swooped into Ravi's sprawling bungalow. The grand Deshmukh *Wada* was nestled just outside the Aarey Forest, the largest and only green strip in the concrete jungle of Mumbai within the eco-sensitive zone of Sanjay Gandhi National Park.

Despite being surrounded by modern civilization, the forest contained a lot of indigenous tribes who worked tirelessly to preserve the fauna and flora of the place. Some even called it the oxygen tank of polluted Mumbai.

Forty-year-old Ravi Deshmukh was revered by all the tribals. Not because he was rich, but because of the great legacy that his forefathers bore. They were known to work hard for the rights and comforts of the tribals.

Unlike Mumbai, the Aarey Forest retired as soon as it turned dark. The inhabitants woke up at dawn and stopped working at dusk. They loved and respected his family.

Eighteen years ago, Suruchi had entered Deshmukh *Wada* as a bride, bringing happiness and prosperity with her. Together, she and Ravi had built a fascinating world for themselves where love conquered all problems, always.

On this fateful morning, Deshmukh *Wada* was covered in a pall of gloom. Every occupant of the forest was shocked at the turn of events. Every eye was wet, mourning the unfortunate passing of their favorite Deshmukh *vaini*, Suruchi.

The worst part was, because of the pandemic restrictions and police presence, no one could visit Ravi's palatial home.

A lady police constable, Rekha Jadhav, was assigned to take care of the children. She was a burly, dark woman with calloused palms and a stern face. Her usually stolid eyes were lined with slight tears when a terrified Rinky clung to her. She wrapped a blanket around the little child and escorted her to the playroom.

Beena had stopped howling and was now sitting on the floor with her knees drawn tightly to her chest. She kept staring at Suruchi's body, which was now wrapped in a clean white sheet.

With great difficulty, the police managed to convince Ravi to get up and sit on the sofa. He was completely dazed and unable to maintain eye contact or communicate. He just kept staring at Suruchi's photograph on the wall.

Dr. Minal Mohite, Suruchi's psychiatrist was also called in, but Ravi was unable to speak to her either. He just broke down and wept hysterically. The police decided to leave him alone and proceed with the rest of the investigation. They found a large number of unconsumed pills below the mattress, and Dr. Mohite confirmed that if Suruchi wasn't taking her medicines, her hallucinations could have escalated.

Conversations with Beena, the neighbors, Omkar and the tribals confirmed that Ravi was a loving husband who would do anything for his family. The police put together the pieces and came to the preliminary conclusion that Suruchi was hallucinating and stuffed the teddy bear in her mouth.

Paralyzed with fear, she may have continued suffocating herself, believing that she was actually somehow freeing herself.

As soon as the cops left, the bell rang. It was Mrs. Chhaya Bapat, the kind, elderly lady from the neighboring bungalow. She had gotten lunch for the family. As per Indian tradition, the home where a death has occurred cannot light the hearth for thirteen days. Relatives and well-meaning friends would take turns and send meals, snacks and hot beverages.

A morose Beena received her at the door. She wasn't surprised to see Mrs. Bapat. Breaking lockdown norms in such situations was common as neighbors in India always looked out for each other in good and bad times. Before her illness, Suruchi spent her afternoons chit-chatting with Mrs. Bapat over cups of steaming hot chai and glucose biscuits. As her illness progressed, her memories of their friendship dwindled, but Mrs. Bapat never gave up on her and regularly visited the Deshmukh *Wada*.

Mrs. Bapat was an attractive, silver-haired health freak and an inspiration to many. She gathered the children and tried to coax them to eat. Beena sighed and fought her tears as she watched Mrs. Bapat trying to get Rinky to speak.

Rinky was sitting on the floor playing with her dolls. Mrs. Bapat sat down beside her and caressed the little one's cheeks.

"What are you doing, *Beta*?" she asked lovingly.

"I am playing with Stacy," Rinky answered in a low voice while combing her doll's hair.

"That's nice. Aren't you hungry? I have cooked your favorite food. *Dal*, rice, *chapati* and *bhindi*! I have also made some *mango kheer*; you love it, don't you?"

Rinky nodded slightly and continued to play with Stacy. Mrs. Bapat gently scooped the little child in her arms and kissed her, placed her at the table and gently persuaded her to eat. Rinky looked at Omkar and signaled him to join her. He ambled towards the table slowly and sat beside his sister.

They ate quietly as Mrs. Bapat and Beena watched them lovingly. After some time, Rinky's sweet voice cut through the stone-cold silence.

"What happened to *Aai*? Omkar dada said she died. Tell me Bapat kaku, what happened to *Aai*?"

Just as Mrs. Bapat opened her mouth to answer, Beena replied hurriedly, "She is with God now. He has made her a star."

Mrs. Bapat and Beena's eyes were filled with tears as they exchanged glances. Omkar gauged their desperation.

He fought the oncoming tears and gulped hard before exclaiming, "Rinky, do you want to hear the latest story I wrote? The end is going to surprise you! However, I cannot tell you till you eat."

He kissed her lovingly while looking at his dad from the corner of his eye.

Rinky exclaimed happily, "Really, *Dada*? Okay! Let's eat! *Baba*! Come, let's eat!"

"*Saheb*, the children need you now and you need the strength," Beena implored Ravi. "Your relatives will be coming soon; you need to eat so that you can handle everyone and everything. Please, *Saheb*, please!"

Ravi threw his hands up in exasperation and spoke softly, "No one is coming, Beena. These are SARS-CoV-2 times; people are skeptical about large gatherings. Besides, the government forbids it. I made Omkar message everyone requesting them to stay home. We will live stream the religious rituals. That way, everyone can pay their respects while being safe."

She kept looking at him with a puppy face. Ravi looked at her, sighed loudly and got up. He slowly sauntered to the table and started nibbling at the *chapati* and vegetables. Mrs. Bapat bade them goodbye quietly and promised to come back soon.

Omkar and Rinky kept Ravi entertained with their jokes and amusing banter through the afternoon. The house was resonating with their happy and playful voices. That's when Ravi realized, for all practical purposes, Suruchi had been absent among them for almost two years, ever since the SARS-CoV-2 pandemic had hit India. An unexplained fear had gripped her and she had regressed into a petrified child. She was completely dependent on Ravi for everything. Her therapy sessions with Dr. Mohite would sometimes last for three hours at a stretch. Apart from that, Ravi helped her with extended passive-therapy sessions that had yoga and deep breathing bundled in.

A large part of his day was spent taking care of his wife. He was home anyway because of the lockdown. However, the more time he spent with her, the less time he was able to give his business, and his business suffered, but he got time to spend with his wife. He loved her a lot and couldn't imagine his life without her. His Suru, his darling Suru.

The phone ring jolted him out of his reverie. It was Samir.

"I am so sorry to hear about Suruchi *vaini*, Ravi. And this may seem like the wrong time, but you need to make a decision about your life, fast."

Samir hardly sounded sorry.

His tone annoyed Ravi and he retorted angrily, "What are you trying to say? For God's sake, it's not even twenty-four hours since I lost my wife. Shut up and hang up, now!"

As the line went blank, Ravi grunted loudly.

"What happened, *Baba*? Come fast, join us!" squealed Rinky.

He went back to the table and nodded slightly with half smiles throughout the lunch.

Later that afternoon, he stood in the hallway staring at the closed door of his bedroom. Even though the police had cleared the room, he couldn't get himself to enter it. It was just too painful. He took a bath in the guest bedroom and wore a set of fresh clothes.

He called out to the kids, "Omkar, Rinky, want to go star-gazing in the forest today? Maybe, we can find your mother among the stars."

He mustered the courage to sound as normal as he could.

Beena started to open her mouth, but Ravi signaled her to keep quiet.

Omkar shrugged and refused, but Rinky started dancing happily.

Ravi smiled weakly and replied, "Okay then, Rinky, let's go! We leave in half an hour, exactly 4 p.m.! Omkar, you can wait back here."

Beena muttered under her breath while packing, "It's not even twenty-four hours since Suruchi *vaini* left us, she is still at the morgue, her last rites are pending…"

Why would this man want to go to the forest, and with the little girl? He has lost it… just like his wife… He has gone mad… just mad! she thought.

After about an hour, the duo set out into the forest in their Jeep. An excited Rinky waved happily at an unhappy Beena and gloomy Omkar, and chatted nonstop while Ravi drove quietly. His mind was clouded and his heart felt empty. He wasn't sure when the axe of bankruptcy would fall on his family as Samir's words kept echoing in his mind, "Decide, Ravi. Decide fast."

The approaching road was dotted with large billboards thanking the government for declaring Aarey as a forest. They remained on the main road, driving through a large awning of shady and dense trees. The umber brown forest was a leafy paradise and driving through it was pure pleasure. The temperatures were always two or three degrees cooler because of the thick and endless canopy of greenery.

The quality of air changed and Ravi noticed Rinky taking in deep breaths. The open Jeep was moving at moderate speed and the wind was playing with her silky brown hair. Her sweet face was glowing with happiness.

She had forgotten her sorrows. Ravi sighed to himself.

Childhood was such a bliss. The ability to live, laugh and forget is so amazing when one is a child.

He unexpectedly applied brakes to allow a deer to pass by. Thankfully, Rinky was wearing a seatbelt. She squealed in happiness and waved at the deer who walked away nonchalantly.

The distinct fragrance of exotic flowers pervaded through the evening air. Far into the horizon, the sun was about to set. The experience was surreal and felt as if the Jeep was driving straight into the scene that was lit up with bright shades of yellow, orange and lavender. The golden rays of the sun were flirting with the trees and the landscape as it invited the evening to take over.

He knew of a secluded spot near the river that offered peace and tranquility to anyone who cared to visit. He parked the Jeep at a distance and held out his hand. Rinky clutched it and jumped out on the grassy terrain.

They sat on the lush green grass near the river and watched the mesmerizing sunset. The dew on the leaves was glistening in the dance of moonlight coming in and sunlight going out. Rinky darted her eyes around as the rustling sounds of small animals scurrying under the thick ferns filled the air. The moon seemed to turn the leaves into a flaming patchwork of colors: scorching yellows, lava reds and burnished browns. It added color to the perfect picnic spot. The cool evening breeze played with her hair as she jumped around trying to catch a butterfly. She yelped in pure delight when she spotted a pair of squirrels chattering on a lush green tree. The birds were singing welcome songs for the moon and the wind was whistling around the trunks causing occasional showers of leaves. Rinky leapt towards the squirrels and screamed loudly when she saw a beetle scrabbling on the tree trunk.

Ravi took a deep breath and looked around; it was peaceful despite the native sounds of the forest. The earthy smell mixed with the aroma of wild flowers allowed peace to enter his troubled heart. He lifted his face letting the evening light and shadows dance across his skin.

Ravi spread out a straw mat and placed the picnic basket on it. It contained peanut butter and jelly sandwiches, grilled chicken, some fruits and juices. Beena had also packed some popcorn that they would roast later. The gurgling sound of the river partnered with the knocks of the hammer as Ravi toiled to put up the tent.

"Wow, *Baba*! This is so amazing! *Baba*, you are my hero! Thank you, *Baba*. Thank you!"

Rinky pranced all around him chanting praises for her father, who seemed a superhero in her eyes. The words were daggers that stabbed Ravi's heart as he looked at her forlornly with a slight smile.

Rinky munched at the sandwiches happily and then laid on the mat, staring into the sky. Night crept in slowly and she shouted in jubilation when the evening star made its appearance.

"Look, *Baba*! It's *Aai*!" she exclaimed joyfully.

Ravi smiled at her and gathered her in his arms. She kept looking at Venus lovingly and smiling happily. One by one, more stars appeared like lucid snowflakes of glinting silver as they sprinkled the night sky. After a while, she placed her little head on his lap, held his hand tightly and dozed off.

He looked at her sweet face, so peaceful and angelic. He set her aside and lay beside her, staring into the sky. It was an unusually clear evening that proceeded into a pitch-black night sky. The beauty of the forest was comforting. A feeling of unexplained peace descended upon his anxious heart. He inhaled the minty fresh air and started humming a popular song from his favorite *Marathi* film.

He walked around the perimeter of the river as the twigs crunched under his feet. The leaves swooshed and he thought he saw a pair of golden eyes looking at him. His heart skipped a beat as he felt a leopard slinking away into the darkness. He sat up promptly and started gathering dried wood to build a campfire. He placed sleeping bags inside the tent and unfolded two chairs and a table. It was time to start prepping for dinner as the portable radio played soulful melodies and he hummed along. While taking a swig at his chilled beer, he closed his eyes to feel the beats and lyrics. Flashes of Suruchi entered his mind's eye, interspersed by Samir's voice booming in the background.

"Make the decision, make it fast!"

His eyes fluttered open.

He sat up and looked around. It was a beautiful night. The pale crescent moon shone like a silvery claw in the night sky. The water glistened in the moonlight and a light breeze played with the leaves. The fire seemed to keep the wildlife away, and the heat seemed to disturb delicate Rinky who was used to the air conditioner. She woke up and started cribbing. He distracted her by pointing at an imaginary herd of deer and the starry sky. He handed over a bowl of grilled chicken and she was thrilled to munch it while talking to her mother among the stars.

They sat there chomping hungrily at the delicious chicken. She sipped juice while her father guzzled beer and told her stories of his childhood, which she listened to intently. He faced a barrage of questions after each story and he patiently answered all of them. After a while, the fire died down and Ravi knew it was time.

He handed over the tablet to his daughter and told her that he was going for a quick tinkle.

"Don't go, *baba*! I am scared!" she wailed.

He hugged her tightly and said tenderly, "Hey, sugar, don't worry! I will be back in no time."

She put out her little finger and asked innocently, "Promise?"

"Yes, promise! I will come back," he locked his little finger in hers and reassured her affectionately.

The dried leaves crunched below his feet as he trudged towards the Jeep, memories of the past flashing by. When Rinky was born, Ravi's *Aai* had insisted that he leave her in the jungle. A girl child was a complete no-no. She cursed Suruchi for her unpardonable mistake and insisted that the forest is where this bad omen belonged. With Suruchi gone, Rinky would have to face insurmountable hardships at the hands of her grandparents.

🌲 🌲 🌲

Ravi was speeding through the forest, the leaves brushing his face and arms through the open Jeep. He was lost in his thoughts when a sharp branch bruised his shoulder, and he winced in pain. He was rudely reminded that his mother wasn't the reason why he left Rinky behind. It was something else. Something he refused to acknowledge.

Rain clouds had gathered in the tar-black sky as Ravi sat in his Jeep. It started raining heavily and the drops lashed angrily at him. The trees crashed against each other like drumsticks in the hands of a giant. A wall of rain stood before him as the drops drummed against the canopy of leaves. The thunder, lightning and heavy rain were blinding. Ravi's heart sank at the thought of little Rinky battling the harsh rain. He fought his tears and the storm while speeding through the forest

She is smart. She will hide in the tent, he thought.

What about the wild animals? The stream is a watering hole frequented by leopards, asked a pesky voice inside his head.

The noise on the hood of the Jeep was like phut-phut-phut just like ripened nuts make when they hit the ground. They seemed to be competing with his heart that was threatening to explode.

He shook his head and exclaimed loudly, "You need to do this, Ravi. It's the decision. You have finally taken it. Stop second-guessing yourself."

She is your daughter and you are all that she has. You, Ravi Deshmukh, are the worst father in the world!

The voice in his head turned louder and angrier.

The car came to a screeching halt as he absentmindedly applied the brakes. With a deep sigh, he rested his head at the steering wheel.

He groaned loudly.

There are so many tribal hamlets in Aarey forest, someone will save her and raise her. Why does it have to be me?

The rain stopped suddenly. He closed his eyes. The breeze had turned strong and howled through the trees. The leaves were rustling noisily and the crickets were buzzing loudly. It was as if all of them had cloaked themselves in the armor of morality.

A swarm of fireflies were dancing in front of his Jeep, and Ravi watched them closely. After a while, he went into a deep trance. He saw himself having fun with Suruchi, Omkar and Rinky.

🌲 🌲 🌲

"You are my lucky charm! Ever since you were born, business has been booming! Thank you, Rinky, my darling! I love you!" He hugged the two-year-old chubby toddler who babbled, "I la boo, *Baba*, I la boo!"

🌲 🌲 🌲

Years later, she had a fall while learning how to ride a bicycle and scraped her knee. "It's okay, sugar, I am here!"

She snuggled close to him and shrieked, "*Baba*! *Baba*! Make it go away, *Baba*… please! It hurts! Ouch!"

He remembered caressing her to sleep for seven nights after that so she felt better. Suruchi and Omkar would gang up and tease him for being such a weakling.

"Rinky has *Baba* wrapped around her little finger," they would quip in laughter.

The breeze had now turned into a wind and a branch cracked and fell on the hood of the Jeep. He jumped out of the Jeep to assess the damage when he felt a tap on his shoulder. Startled, he turned to find a craggy face staring right at him. He stepped back and almost slipped on a stone.

"Oh, Ravi *Saheb, sambhala swatahala*. I mean, take care, *Saheb*."

His voice was like a foghorn that cut through the silence and stung Ravi's ears.

As Ravi balanced himself, he looked at the stranger dressed in a traditional white *dhoti* and torn brown shirt; a white turban adorned his head. A hood made of straw acted as a raincoat and offered some protection from the harsh rain. He held a lantern in his left hand and a thick stick in the other. A little girl, slightly older than Rinky, was perched on his shoulders like a monkey. Her tired eyes peeped at Ravi from under the straw hood. He stood there, barefoot staring at Ravi with utmost respect in his bug eyes. He hovered around as if he was awaiting instructions from the famous Ravi *Saheb*.

Ravi was in no mood for salutations and ignored him. He got into the Jeep and turned on the ignition, but the Jeep refused to start.

"Urgh!" he growled.

The tribal man spoke in a heavily accented voice.

"*Saheb*, your … car… must be… hot… I mean… to say, overhotted. Check spark plug now… see…"

Ravi looked at him and nodded impatiently.

"I the Tukaram Bhoir, from *Devicha Pada*. You remember me? Last year, during *Devi Pooja*, I was standing at temple gate. You and *vaini* had smiled at me and given me a bag of grains."

He gave him a wide grin while Ravi looked at him quizzically.

The tribal man shook his head and chuckled nervously.

"I so silly. How you big man remember me, I the Tukaram. Huh? Not possible only. I thinking silly manner. No?"

Lightning struck one of the trees and another branch came crashing down right behind them. Ravi's heart sank. Rinky must be so afraid right now. He started rubbing his palms nervously.

"What happened, *Saheb*? All ok? I help. I call village friends?"

Tukaram stepped forward. Ravi stepped back and shouted angrily.

"What is your problem? Why don't you just leave?"

Tukaram moved away meekly and spoke hesitantly.

"*Saheb*, we all heard about *vaini*… I know you upset… I cannot take away pain of loss… but I can help for Jeep… if you wish…"

Ravi composed himself as Tukaram turned to check on his daughter.

"Is she your daughter? What are you doing here so late at night?" Ravi enquired curiously.

"Yes, this daughter mine, Vanu, Vanita. She lost walking. Something… polio… doctor told. But our *vaidyaraja* said she walk fast again. Soon."

Ravi nodded and smiled slightly. Tukaram continued, his voice was laced with love and affection for his daughter.

"My Vanu, she *lai hushaar*, what you say – intalligent? Yes, my Vanu bery intalligent. And if she walk, then she study and become big officer in big big office. I take to *vaidyaraja* every day for, what you say, tritment?"

Ravi's curiosity was mounting.

"You mean treatment? Yes, but isn't she heavy? Polio cannot be cured. Your vaidyaraja is fooling you."

Tukaram smiled and replied in a pragmatic tone.

"What to say… I mean… I her *Baba*—she think I hero, can do magic. Hahaha… all village friends think *vaidyaraja* is magician. He cure anyone all times they tell"

He set aside the lantern and stick, folding his hands in respect as he continued in his deep-throated voice.

"What to do, *Saheb*? Vanu… my daughter, what you say… pride? She my lucky charm. She born and only happiness come home."

He turned to look at her lovingly. His face had a warm glow, and she smiled back happily at her father.

He spoke slowly. "Yes, money problem, but *Devi* ensuring that we hardly hungry. What heavy, *Saheb*? Pray, tell me, own children, how be heavy for us? We blessed to be parent. *Devi* bless us. My Vanu is light as a flower for me... not at all heavy. She my daughter, my life…my… what you say… my joy!"

It started raining again. The little girl started whimpering. Tukaram shushed her tenderly. He bent slightly and gathered his lantern and stick while perfectly balancing Vanita. He smiled at Ravi and bade him goodbye before disappearing into the dark forest.

His words had pierced Ravi's conscience and shook him to the core.

Tukaram was right! How can one's own children be a burden on a parent?

Ravi braced himself, and this time, his resolve was stronger than steel. He had made his decision.

He climbed into the Jeep, and it magically started. He turned it around and went back to the campsite, but the tent was empty and Rinky was nowhere to be seen.

Oh, my goodness! Where could she be!

He was about to shout, when he heard a low roar. Not as loud as a lion, but more like a short pur. His heart sank.

A leopard!

His heart was beating very fast and he whispered a million prayers in a single breath. Now he didn't want to lose his daughter, ever again.

Far ahead, behind a tree, he could hear a low whistle. His heart leaped in pure joy. It was their signal! Rinky was alive and behind the trees somewhere. He looked around and saw a small cave, the whistle coming from inside it.

Happy tears were rolling down his cheeks as he whistled back. He could feel a pair of glowing eyes staring at him, and he didn't move until the leopard moved away first. He knew that leopards could see seven times better than humans, but if he didn't appear threatening, it would leave him alone.

Once it seemed safe, he stealthily approached the cave. It was dark and damp. His torch penetrated through the darkness, and his heart was beating loudly and threatening to jump out of his mouth.

As he stepped in, his shoes shuffled over the floor as the fluttering of bat wings echoed through the cave. He bent down to avoid bumping his head on the low ceiling. The briny smell of slimy lichen made him wince. He held his breath to avoid the stale air from stinging his nostrils.

The stone walls were covered with moss and water was dripping from the cracks and crevices. Huge cobwebs covered the corners. The floor was dirty and strewn with tree roots, dead leaves, twigs, trash and campfire remains.

He grasped the knobby walls to avoid tripping over the debris and stones.

His heart was racing as he asked himself, *Was this the home of a leopard?*

He chided himself for not carrying a stick with him.

He controlled his breathing and let out their signature whistle once again. A colony of bats emerged from the interiors, he dropped the torch and started fighting them with his bare hands. He screamed in pain as they left. It was a tough fight that left bleeding scratch marks on his rugged face.

Drops of blood mixed with sweat were trickling down his face as he groped in the dark and found the torch. Thankfully, it wasn't damaged. He picked it up and let out their signature whistle. He was overjoyed when she responded with the same whistle once again.

He spotted her behind a boulder.

"Rinky, Rinky!" he whispered hoarsely.

"*Baba*?" she said in a low voice. "Is that you, *Baba*?"

He replied lovingly, "Yes, sugar! It's me, your *Baba*!"

"*Baba*!" she screamed and sprung into his arms.

He hugged her tightly.

"I knew you would come, you promised me… you did… you would never break our pinky promise," she babbled excitedly.

He nodded happily, "Yes, sugar… let's go back home. Shall we?"

"No! No, *Baba*! I wished at a falling star tonight when you were gone. I am sure, *Aai* will talk back as a star tonight! I have to wait and watch!" she quipped eagerly.

He smiled and nodded.

They emerged from the cave and sat talking for a while. She gathered small rounded pebbles and threw them into the river. He poked at the fire and the popcorn crackled in the midnight silence. After that, they slept in the tent and it was the most peaceful sleep Ravi had had in days.

They woke up the next morning and drove back to Deshmukh *Wada*. His mother was there to welcome them at the gate. She started crying when she saw them approach. He was surprised at her hypocrisy. She had hated Suruchi her entire life. And now that she was gone, *Aai*'s heart must be jumping in joy and she was doing a fabulous job at hiding it.

"How are you, Ravi *Beta*? It shouldn't have happened! Now, my grandkids are without a mother" she shed crocodile tears while hugging him.

"Don't worry, *Aai*, I will take care of the kids. They are mine too, remember?" he told her confidently.

Rinky jumped into Omkar's arms and all three of them hugged each other.

Then, the phone rang. It was Samir.

"We will get Suruchi's life insurance. What about Rinky? Did you make the decision?" asked Samir.

"Samir, one sacrifice to SARS-CoV-2 is enough. My Rinky doesn't deserve to get caught in a financial crossfire. I have decided. My lucky charm will help me succeed."

Ravi disconnected and closed his eyes.

Flashes appeared once again; Suruchi begging for death, him scattering pills below the mattress and then stuffing the teddy bear into her mouth. She had thanked him with gratitude in her eyes. She wanted her death and he needed it. Her life insurance, fifty million rupees, was going to be a life-saver for the family and, according to Samir, getting rid of Rinky would give him an additional twenty million and solve all problems for a long time. However, he just couldn't do it, not to his own offspring.

Rinky just didn't deserve it but then, did Suruchi?

Beyond the truth, lies reality. The truth was that Suruchi was headed towards doom anyways and the reality was that Ravi and the children needed the insurance money.

Ravi opened his eyes, looked at his children and hugged them tightly as they hugged him back. He made a quiet resolve to ensure that Suruchi's sacrifice didn't go to waste.

GLOSSARY:

Aai: Mother.

Baba: Daddy.

Beta: Child.

Chai: Tea.

Chapati: Flat wheat bread.

Dada: Elder brother.

Dal: Lentil curry.

Devi: Goddess.

Devi Pooja: An annual festival held to worship a goddess.

Devicha Pada: A hamlet in Aarey Forest.

Dhoti: A traditional men's garment worn in India.

Egg bhurji: Scrambled eggs.

Kaku: Auntie.

Kheer: A chilled Indian dessert made from slow-cooked rice or vermicelli, milk, and sugar.

Lai hushaar: Very intelligent.

Madam: Madame or Master.

Marathi: A style of film in Indie; also called *Mollywood*.

Saheb: Sir or Master.

Sambhala swatahala: Take care of yourself.

Sari: A garment consisting of a length of cotton or silk elaborately draped around the body.

Vaidyaraja: A healer of the village believed to have knowledge of herbs and magical cures.

Vaini: Sister-in-law.

Wada: Mansion.

For When You're Ready To Say Goodbye

By

Kaina Lisibach

It has been over a decade since I last saw my sister.

One hundred and twenty-two months with only the ghost of her memory in the place her bright presence used to be. That's all I can think about as I park my dad's car in Yosemite National Park. The last time I visited this place was with her.

A week ago, I woke up with an inexplicable restlessness that stirred me from sleep at three in the morning. I had turned to my left on instinct, where her bed used to be in the room we shared in a house with four bedrooms. My mouth was parted in mid-sentence when I remembered, recalled the fact that, in a few days, it would officially be another year without her.

I couldn't get out of bed for the rest of the day after that.

But the urge to do something lingered. I thought cleaning every habitable space of dust would help, and I had made my way through most of the house when I found it at the bottom of my drawer—right where I had shoved it years ago after failing to open it yet again. And it was then, holding the letter in one hand and a pink and purple feather duster in the other, that it finally felt right.

So, here I am, looking down at the envelope that made me get on a plane and drive all the way to Yosemite, the paper wrinkled by age and fold marks. Written on it in a messy scrawl: *For when you're ready to say goodbye.*

I take a deep breath. I don't think I ever would be. The finality of the message had made me hide this last piece of her for years, in denial, a stark contrast to the eager anticipation I felt for all the other letters in the box she gifted me. For when you turn eighteen; *for when you start college; for when you get your heart broken for the first time; for when you meet someone; for when you graduate; for when you fuck up; for when you get married; for when you're questioning everything.* On and on they went. The gift of her words on every milestone, big and small, were so consistent that, sometimes, it felt like she hadn't left at all.

Yet, this. This I always dreaded, the thought of it a whisper at the back of my mind each time I excitedly tore open a new one. The inevitable moment I would get to this one. The very last one.

If I didn't open it, I could just continue to pretend that she was off somewhere far away, sending me letters as she made her way across continents like we had always planned, that any day now she would walk through my door. But it had been ten years since she'd passed. The wishful thinking and denial felt like a sweater a size too small, outgrown and in need of disposal during spring cleaning.

For when you're ready to say goodbye. I trace my fingertips over the words. Her handwriting really was awful, the letters thrown together like she was rushing to put it all down so she could move on to something else. I had learned to decipher it thanks to the years of being the first reviewer of whichever story she had stayed up all night frantically jotting down.

Beneath it, written smaller in bold letters with a very aggressive underline read:

"P.S. To only be opened at our favorite place!"

Leave it to Sage to be a pain in the ass even from beyond the grave. I had instantly known the recipient of such an esteemed accolade, a presence so constant it might as well have been another member of our family of three—the forest. This forest, specifically.

Dad started to bring us both along before we could even walk. He was a venture capitalist Monday through Friday and a nature lover with one foot in the wilderness whenever he managed to hide his laptop away. After every drive down, he would get out of the car and take one deep ceremonial breath, a huge, beautiful smile marking the official point that he left all his troubles in the driver seat of his Land Rover.

"Feel that, girls?" he would ask us. "The mountains are calling."

He had cultivated that same love within us, indulging us in our every curiosity, motivating any sort of interest in outdoor-related activities. While our friends did violin and summer prep programs, we did mountain biking, Girl Scouts, kayaking, fishing. Rock climbing, however, had been the one that stuck out the most. Dad taught us everything he knew, and it led us to championships and world cups. But the awards were never the driving reason I kept at it.

Sage was the one driven by the winning, I was just happy to be there, conquering mountains with my sister.

I get out of the car and, on instinct, my lungs take a big, long breath, the scent of pine trees filling me, instantly making me feel at home. And suddenly I am fifteen again. I can easily see my dad's smile. I can see Sage indulging him in the practice while discretely rolling her eyes at me in amusement. The memory of it sends a pang of heartache through my chest, and I am abruptly hit with a deep longing for my dad. The ringing of my phone snaps me out of it, and my lips rise as I see who it is.

"You know, it's freaky when you do that."

"Do what?" my father asks, the sound of dishes and running water in the background. "Hear me thinking from miles away."

"The mountains alerted me of your arrival."

"More like Find My iPhone, but I'll go along with it," I tell him with a smile as I lean back against the car.

The sound of water stops, and I can feel him turn all his attention to me.

"How are you feeling?" he asks, dad mode clearly activated.

"I'm fine."

He says nothing, but his waiting silence says everything. The negotiation strategy he uses at work is one he has employed often in parenting, but I will not crack. I refuse.

It is over when it becomes so loud I start hearing the sound of my own heartbeat.

"I'm fine. Anxious. Nervous. Sad. I imagine them to be very unoriginal emotions when hearing from one's deceased sister for the last time."

"I wish I was there with you, Iris."

He's feeling nice today. I know he can see right through me, but is letting me off easy.

"So do I, Dad, but I have to do this alone, you know that."

"I know," he says with a sigh. "Do you have all your equipment? Have you double-checked everything?"

"You know I have."

Still, he makes me verbally check all of it again with him. I stop him when he tries to do it for a second time.

"Stop it, you mother hen. Everything is good. Just because I'm professionally retired doesn't mean I'm inept."

"Better to be safe than—"

"Splattered on the ground like a pancake," I say with him. "Yes, I know."

"You don't have to be a smartass about it."

"Says the man who used extreme fear tactics on small children to ensure safety compliance."

"Well, you're in one piece, so it was effective on some level, wasn't it?"

"I guess."

"You should get going, you don't want to leave after the sun rises."

"You're right," I tell him as I note the time and push myself off the car.

"I always am… Say hi to her for me, will you?"

I blink away the sudden onslaught of fragile emotion that fills me.

"I will," I say softly. "Love you."

"Love you, sweetheart. Text me when you're on your way back."

I put away my phone and quickly gather everything, the weight of my backpack a little heavier than I remember. The hiking pack is familiar, unchanged even after all these years. Rays of the early morning sun penetrate the towering sequoias, basking the ground with a golden green glow. There is no sound other than that of the forest inhabitants. It is magical.

For our family, this had been a solace. An extraordinary place that felt like it had been made just for us. As I approach the official start of the path, I reach into the pocket of my light jacket and pull out Sage's letter. I take a deep breath as I stare down at it, turning it over and over in my hands. With shaking fingers, I finally break open the envelope and pull out the letter.

Dear Iris,

I thought this one might be better to hear.

With all my love,

Sage

Completely confused, I simply stand there for a few seconds. There is no way she made this so anticlimactic.

That's when I see that there is something else in the envelope. I turn it upside down and a small audio player slides out. With still-shaking fingers, I press the play button.

"Hey, Ri."

My eyes instantly water at the sound of her voice. It takes one, two, three blinks before I can breathe over the lump in my throat.

"I'm so happy you're here. Consider this my motivational introduction. Start walking, you've got a long way to go. I even curated a tasteful playlist for your enjoyment. Bye."

An eight-mile hike to the mountains, with only my thoughts as company and no choice but to think about Sage. Lovely.

Sleep On The Floor by The Lumineers comes on and I am transported to the back of my dad's Land Rover, windows open, Sage sitting beside me with a radiant smile as the wind blows through our hair. Moments like that, when peaceful contentment came easy, were now elusive. The echo of the feeling felt more like fiction than reality.

I spent a long time trying to find it again in places, trekking from one new city to another like it would fill up the void I felt, but it was on top of some World Wonder, with that feeling in my chest no less overwhelming, that I realized it was her. The space she had left behind. And it wouldn't go away for the rest of my life.

A family of four draws me out of my thoughts. The scenic picture of them beneath the soaring sequoias disturbed by the raised voices of the older girl and younger brother. I smile in greeting and I can feel it burgeoning into a grin as I take in the antics of the siblings. The parents are chiding them to stop arguing, but it is obvious by their exaggerated eye rolls and fake sighs of annoyance that their behavior is all in jest. A second later, they dissolve into laughter over whatever it is that they were fighting about, instantly on good terms again. The easy camaraderie is so familiar that my smile slowly wanes.

The last days were the hardest. I remember looking at her once—really looking at her—while they pumped her body full of chemo. Her face, identical to my own, was drawn and swollen, hair long gone. I don't know why, but it actually sunk in then—that she was dying and there was no stopping it.

My brilliant, caring, hilarious, older sister was dying. There was no god I could pray to, no doctor I could track down to fix it. A concerned look appeared on her face when she realized where my thoughts had gone. I didn't even have to say anything—Sage just knew.

"I can't do this," I told her as I tried to blink away the tears that seemed to emerge all the time those days. "I can't do any of this without you."

"Iris…." she said softly as she wiped my tears away and took my face in her hands, fortitude peeking through her tired eyes. "You can and you will."

It seemed like we were constantly trading strength back then, taking turns being the one who kept the other from falling apart.

I snuck away while she was sleeping to track down her Oncologist. I'm her twin sister, isn't there anything I can give? Donate? Stem cells or something? The kind-eyed doctor had given me a sympathetic look. No, honey, there's nothing you can do. I would have happily offered her the very air in my lungs if it would have eased any fragment of her pain.

But I couldn't. Once the treatments stopped working, the doctors told Dad and me to prepare ourselves. All we can do is make her comfortable now. I wanted to scream. I wanted to rip apart all their clipboards, strip the clinical detached look in their eyes. That is my sister, I wanted to yell.

I was so mad then. Mad at the world. Mad at the doctors. Mad at Sage for dying. Mad at Dad for giving me a twin I could lose. Mad at Mom for not being alive for any of it.

Sage passed away at 3:15 a.m. on May 10th at Roosevelt Regional Hospital. I was holding one hand while Dad held the other. When the force of his sobs shook the bed I just sat there, unable to move as I waited for her eyes to flutter open again, a numbness spreading through me when I realized they never would.

She was seventeen.

I don't remember much of what happened after. I can't recall a lot of the funeral or the months that followed. But I do remember the first time we went home. The hushed silence as Dad and I stood frozen at the door as we took in the long hallway of framed family pictures. Sage was everywhere. In the Sylvia Plath books left on the nightstand, the National Geographic magazines sprawled across the living room table, the unopened college acceptance letters on the counter.

The echo of her absence was resounding. It made me think about all the things she wouldn't be there for. The favorite songs that would no longer have a second singer, all the events that would go on without an accomplice.

I remember the guilt that struck me often in the months after, so potent that it felt like I was choking. Our first birthday after she passed was one of the worst days of my life. My dad pretended like his hands weren't shaking as he brought over a cake with eighteen candles. I acted as if I didn't spend the rest of the night sobbing into my pillow thinking about how my only wish could never possibly come true.

Whichever universal force had deemed it appropriate for one twin to go on without the other seemed particularly cruel on every July 3rd.

I came to the conclusion that everyone had reasons. For living, I mean. A dream, a job, children, a partner, money, parents, and on and on. Reasons that justified staying on a floating rock where the bad often outnumbered the good. For most of my life, Sage made up so many of those reasons that I had never even contemplated another version of reality.

How do you keep going when 90% of your reasons go off and disappear?

So much of my identity was composed of everything that was connected to her. The never-ending questions and resulting insomnia became part of my new long-term best friends group. Friends that took years of expensive therapy to wade through. I had to reshape myself around the hole she had left behind. Heal jaggedly around the edges that still hurt to touch, even now.

🌲 🌲 🌲

Hours later, Half Dome comes into view, and I am hit with just a bit of nervousness. It is easy to forget the risk of falling to your death when you are a teenager looking for an adrenaline rush. It is not as simple when you're nearing thirty. As I take in the immense mountain, I start to wonder whether Sage would even know if I played the recording from the safety of the ground when the playlist stops.

"Okay, put me back on when you're at the top." Her voice is a welcome change from my somber thoughts, reminding me that while she may be gone, I still have this with her. "I'm setting the timer on for three hours. If you take longer than that, I'm going to be shaking my head from all the way here."

I click the recording off. She was crazy. A three-hour climb was something we would do when we were at our peak, seventeen with meticulously optimized stamina. Years after easing off the rigorous training and very much not seventeen, there is no way I can finish so quickly. Regardless, I can still feel my competitiveness springing up at the thought of it, which is why I know she posed the challenge in the first place.

I take out all my equipment and prepare myself to start climbing. Chalking up my hands, I look up and I am greeted by hundreds of feet of unyielding rock. Despite it being years since I withdrew from the sport, I still frequent an indoor gym to avoid losing my ability to do this again if I ever wanted to. But I haven't climbed an actual mountain in a decade. Not without her.

It feels weird to even think about it, like doing it without an arm. I shut my mind off as I take that first step and then the next and the one after that. Until I am well above the ground and there is no going back. I happily give myself over to the physical exertion. Suspended on the side of a mountain, there is nothing to focus on except what my body is doing. It provides a welcome reprieve from the loudness of my thoughts.

The minutes become hours, the sun is unwavering at my back and it feels as if even my eyeballs are burning. Somehow, I make it to the top, arms buckling as I pull myself over. I collapse on the ground, giving myself a few minutes to catch my breath. It is there, on the dirt and about to heave my guts out, that I gather the courage to press play again.

"You were slow," Sage teases. I snort and my eyes roll automatically.

She pauses and takes a deep breath. "Hi there, little sister," Sage says gently.

My heart clenches. This is going to wreck me; I can feel it.

"You must be wondering why I brought you here. A beach might have been easier, more cinematic even. But, while I wish I could claim some commitment to being a pain in the ass that transcends life itself, I thought that if there was any place you and I could say goodbye, it would be here."

I squeeze my eyes shut, allowing the sound of her voice to steady me. Force my breaths in and out.

"I am here by the way." She stops as if waiting. I patiently stand by for the philosophical rant about death not being the end. "No, Iris, like actually here, turn around."

My eyes snap open, and I slowly raise half my body off the ground, heart racing even as I know it is impossible. All I see is a whole lot of shrubbery and an out-of-place looking tree.

"You see that sexy gorgeous tree? That's me." My eyes dart back to the Western White Pine that I had quickly dismissed. No way. A snicker escapes me before I can stop it. It was such a Sage thing to do. Ridiculous and enduring all at once. My shoulders start to shake with the force of my laughter, half-listening and half-trying to prevent tears from forming. "What in the world did you do?" I manage to get out despite my cackling.

"At least, I hope it's a tree by now. I have no idea how long it has been. I made Dad find one of those tree urn companies. Dying wishes and whatnot. You should have seen his face when I asked him," she tells me with a giggle that soon transforms into roaring laughter. At the sound of her ugly snorting, I lose it. The ring of our combined howling is so familiar that I tuck a piece of it away. Nothing to see here, just two sisters in hysterics as usual.

"I'm sorry, I'm sorry," she wheezes, making the corners of my mouth rise as my laughter calms down. "I know this is supposed to be serious or whatever, but I can't believe I'm dying, dude. This feels like a mediocre Lifetime movie. Cut the cameras!" she exclaims dramatically.

I shake my head, smiling wide in response to her theatrics. I had forgotten the vibrancy of her spirit, the intonation of her humor and the comfort of her presence during the years that I only had her letters.

"Anyways, the point is, that's me. Take a seat and admire the view, it put Dad back a grand."

I do just that. I lean against it and take in the trees spanning for miles, every crevice and dip on the horizon, allowing myself to bask in the warmth of the sun. Here, it is so easy to conceptualize how small I am in the grand scheme of things. I can almost see the life that extends deep beneath the ground at my feet, pulsing to the rhythm of something ethereal and ancient.

On one of our many climbs, I had told Sage that it was on this mountain that I came the closest to believing in any sort of divine power. She'd smiled, ever the believer to my skeptic. It makes sense. It's all connected. It's easier to see that from up here.

"It really is something, isn't it?" she asks, her voice full of awe, reverence evident as if she is sitting here taking it all in with me.

"It really is," I murmur.

"Iris...." she lets out a shuddering breath and I know we have arrived to the serious programming of the day. "I can only imagine what you have been feeling and I am so sorry that you had to go through this alone, but it's time to let go, Ri. Of the parts that no longer serve you. Not of me. If you forget me, I'll haunt you. But the painful bits, the parts that hurt." She pauses, and I can feel her steeling herself for whatever it is she wants to say.

"I love you and I miss you and I know without a doubt," her voice cracks, "that we'll see each other again. But until then, I expect you to live twice as fully. As largely as you possibly can. I want you to be overwhelmingly, disgustingly happy, so you can tell me all about it when I see you. I'm tired of carrying the weight of our entertainment for so many years," she requests with a laugh. "Promise," she says softly.

I can't open my mouth.

"Iris," she chides in her familiar tyrannical voice.

I wipe my nose. My eyes roll as conditioned to in the presence of that tone.

"I promise," I say begrudgingly.

"Good," Sage says, satisfied. And in that instant, the conversation feels so real that my eyes start to water.

"Do you have any good stories to share? This will probably be the only time you'll be able to talk uninterrupted."

"I…." Where to start? There were over ten years of questionable life choices and emotional baggage to sort through and explain.

"Oh my god," she gasps like the thought just occurred to her, "Are you still competing? Are you married right now? Do you have kids? Please tell me you at least traveled before all of that."

There was the year of me going off the rails after she died. Abandoning rock climbing. Going to college. Dropping out of college to see the countries we had always dreamed about. The sort of healing that had come from that. The realization that the acute pain of her loss would be permanent. My career. Meeting Matt. Unexpectedly falling in love. Getting married. The yearning for my own little family. The years of fertility issues.

"It's a lot," I oversimplify.

Sage expels a resigned sigh, "I wish I could teleport for a minute so I could hear about it. It would be like looking into a crystal ball."

I start to respond when something moves at the edge of my vision, and my eyes snap to a blue butterfly fluttering around. The back of my neck tingles at the sight of it. I watch as it inches closer and closer until it settles on my shirt, right on my stomach. I freeze, a sense of awareness raising the hairs on my arm.

My period has been late for three weeks. I had been itching to take a pregnancy test before coming, but I didn't want to get my hopes up. There is no way.

Later, I would find out that I was pregnant. With twin girls.

But right now, it seems like too much of a coincidence. A manifestation of wishful thinking. Until the butterfly flies away and lands on a bed of flowers I hadn't noticed before.

May Night Sage.

My eyes widen in shock, and I start to cry in earnest, a messy combination of tears and laughter. I can see it then, the look on her face, eyebrows raised. See, you non-believer, there are no coincidences.

"Wherever it is that we go, know that I'm thinking of you. That I'm with you, no matter where in the world you are." I can hear her tearing up, the traces of humor disappearing as if she too realizes what is coming.

I suddenly see her everywhere. In the way the trees sway to an invisible song. In the sunlight that caresses the top of my head, like a warm smile from somewhere far away. All around me, she is there.

I am struck by the overwhelming certainty of her presence, even if I can't physically see her. She's crying and I'm crying and we are a mess of emotions separated by more than a decade worth of time.

"I feel so lucky to have known you, to have been your sister."

I close my eyes as I prepare myself for what's about to happen. The impending finality of it is evident. I hear the sound of curses and complaints in the background.

"That's you and Dad coming up. I have to go before you hear me and discover my grand surprise."

The image of her alive and just seventeen on this very same spot waiting for us to hurry up is overwhelming.

"This is not the end, Ri. Not for us." I can hear her take a trembling breath and I brace myself with every ounce of my being. "I love you and I'm with you, Iris. Always."

With that, the recording ends and there is only silence. Crushing unbearable silence.

I start crying again, sobs so potent I feel like they're going to break me in half. And I see us. As giggling little girls running around barefoot while our dad yells at us to be careful. On every birthday blowing out candles at the same time and sharing the first piece of cake. As young teenagers waking up in the early hours of the morning to train, elbows linked as we plotted how we were going to sneak out to a party later. On graduation day as I push her wheelchair across the stage, Dad in the audience cheering and crying at the same time. I see our triumphs and our failures, all the pinky promises and uncontrollable laughter. And love, so much love and happiness as we navigated this world together.

An honor to live it, a privilege to remember.

Eventually, my body calms down. In that moment, as I revel in equal parts grief and joy and reminisce about all the brightness she left behind, something within me settles and it becomes a little easier to inhale.

I'm with you, Iris. Always.

I'm not sure how much time passes. Maybe, it is minutes or hours, but I somehow find the strength to stand up. I wipe my tears and fix my equipment, preparing everything I need to descend. As I strap myself in and stand on the edge of the mountain, I take one last look at the flourishing pine, comforted by the knowledge that this piece of her will be here forever. At our favorite place.

"Goodbye, Sage," I say with a quivering smile, "I'll see you later."

I release a deep, shaky breath and I let go.

Meet The Authors

KaliVictoria is an American author, currently known for her contribution to angel lore within fantasy literature. Drawn to novels from a young age, KaliVictoria took her love for storytelling a step further in college, making 2020 the year of her literary debut, to which she self-published, *The Shadows of Heaven*, book one within the *Trials of Fate* series. For more information and her works, visit www.kalivictoria.com.

Terry Lander is a British author, best known for his novels *Banned* and *Alf & Mabel*. He started writing in 2005 and has explored a number of different genres, often focusing on the unpredictability of human nature and the emotive side of his characters. In 2017, Terry wrote his first children's book, *Natalie's Fiendish New Headteacher*, which has since become the *Natalie Underwood* trilogy. He has also collaborated with Jamie Arron on a futuristic novella for children titled *Lewis and Bruno Face the Artificial Intelligents*.

MEET THE AUTHORS

DALILA FUENTES is a Mexican-American author, artist, and creative known for her LGBTQ+ fiction stories amongst her loyal readers. She mainly writes dark romance and erotica with a side of fantasy and is currently working on an erotic werewolf romance on Inkitt and Wattpad. Dalila is from sunny California, living with a cat, a dog, and her family. She is currently working on her BA in Liberal Studies and works with small children as a tutor. Her Wattpad is _daylaylay_16.

FLOR ANA is a Cuban-American poet, author, editor and creative best known for her poetry collections *Perspective (and other poems)* and *The Language of Fungi & Flowers*. She continues to write and loves to be out in nature or exploring the world through travel or reading. For more about Flor, check out her Instagram: @littleearthflower or her website, www.littleearthflower.com.

MEET THE AUTHORS

KIM RASHIDI is a Canadian author and the poet behind *Fortunate,* a book of poetry based on tarot. She explores the cosmos through her words and has a soft spot for capturing love and life in the mundane. Writing about the lives, cities, and timelines that mirror back the romantic, she weaves reality with imagined possibilities. She holds an MA in English Literature and has taken to poetry since she was 16. Follow her on Instagram, @kimrashidi, to read her poetry.

JANELLE GIANNETTA is an American writer that debuts as an author in the anthology *Stories From The Forest.* She enjoys writing about the beauties of nature and the creative imagination in which fiction allows. She is currently working on her first novel, which is a work of fiction centered around a young man in his twenties who deals with loss, love, and overcoming difficulties. She is also extremely grateful to be able to share the inner workings of her mind.

MEET THE AUTHORS

MONICA SINGH is a dyed-in-the-wool bibliophile. Her love of reading has led to her passion for writing. She writes so others can find comfort and understanding in her words, just like she has in the words of so many others before her. Her stories are part of several anthologies including, *Tea With a Drop of Honey*, *TRAIL XIII: The Path to Perdition*, and now *Stories From The Forest*. Monica's debut novel *The Pause* published September 2021. She lives in Mumbai, India, with her loving husband, Rahul, and a gentle ginger tomcat named Loki.

KEANU JOAQUIN DEL TORO is an American writer, making his literary debut in *Stories From The Forest*. Hailing from the Sunshine State, Keanu wrote for his school paper and recently graduated with his BA in Creative Writing and a Minor in Film Studies. His short stories revolve around the misadventures of angsty teens and twenty-somethings, while his poetry focuses on the little things and the big things in life: love, depression, Uncrustables, paradise lost and found, and more. His debut poetry collection, *The Eve of Our Generation,* releases December 2021 with Indie Earth Publishing.

MAYURA AMARKANT is an Indian author best known for her internationally praised anthology, *Trapped In Heaven & other stories.* She loves writing fiction and admits that she enjoys spending time with her characters in her head before giving them form on paper. Her blog, DiaryOfAnInsaneWriter.com, is among the top 30 lifestyle blogs in India, according to FeedSpot. Given a choice, Mayura will retire from her successful career as an entrepreneur and focus on writing fiction. She cherishes the dream of becoming a writer for films, TV, and OTT.

MEET THE AUTHORS

KAINA LISIBACH is a Venezuelan-American writer, creative, and entrepreneur. A lifelong lover of stories, her passion for novels led her to start One Page Closer in 2016, a nonprofit initiative that provided fully stocked bookcases to children and teens in low-income communities in her hometown of Miami, Florida. When she's not working as a product marketer at Google, you can find her writing with her favorite G2 pen, traveling, using her camera, or pulling an all-nighter to finish a good book. Learn more about her creative work at www.kainalisibach.com.